Secrets at St Jude's

www.rbooks.co.uk

Also by Carmen Reid

Secrets at St Jude's: New Girl

for adult readers:

The Personal Shopper
Did the Earth Move?
Three in a Bed
Up All Night
How Was it For You?
Late Night Shopping

Secrets at St Jude's

Jealous Girl

CORGI BOOKS

SECRETS AT ST JUDE'S: JEALOUS GIRL
A CORGI BOOK 978 0 552 55707 8

Published in Great Britain by Corgi Books,
an imprint of Random House Children's Books
A Random House Group Company

This edition published 2009

1 3 5 7 9 10 8 6 4 2

The Random House Group Limited supports the Forest Stewardship Council
(FSC), the leading international forest certification organization. All our titles
that are printed on Greenpeace-approved FSC-certified paper carry the FSC
logo. Our paper procurement policy can be found at
www.rbooks.co.uk/environment.

Set in 12/16pt Minion by
Falcon Oast Graphic Art Ltd.

Corgi Books are published by Random House Children's Books,
61–63 Uxbridge Road, London W5 5SA

www.kidsatrandomhouse.co.uk
www.rbooks.co.uk

Addresses for companies within The Random House Group Limited
can be found at: www.randomhouse.co.uk/offices.htm

THE RANDOM HOUSE GROUP Limited Reg. No. 954009

A CIP catalogue record for this book is available from the British Library.

Printed in the UK by CPI Bookmarque, Croydon, CR0 4TD

MEET THE ST JUDE'S GIRLS . . .

GINA

Full name: Gina Louise Winklemann-Peterson

Home: A fabulous white and glass, architect-designed beach house with pool on the Californian coast

Likes: Sunshine (sadly not often found in Edinburgh), swimming, Halloween, pointy ankle boots, Prada or anything Prada-esque, Reece's Pieces, her cell phone, her little brother Menzie (sometimes), coffee, a certain charming part-time waiter at the Arts Café called Dermot O'Hagan

Dislikes: Slithery octopus-type kisses, the totally gross sludge-green St Jude's school uniform, deadly dull history lessons, Charlie Fotherington-whatsit, boiled vegetables of any kind (I mean, guys, like, haven't you heard of stir-fry?)

Would like to be: A screenwriter – but absolutely no one in the whole world knows about that

Fascinating fact: Gina has three other best friends at her old school in California – Paula, Ria and Maddison. They still can't believe she goes to boarding school in Scotland

NIFFY

Full name: Luella Edith Millicent Pethurer Nairn-Bassett (no wonder she's called either 'Niffy' or 'Lou')

Home: The ancient crumbling ancestral mansion Blacklough Hall in Cumbria, England

Likes: Playing pranks, enormous horses and slobbery dogs, all team games (especially hockey – she's really good) the St J's assembly game Banshee Buzzword Bingo (which she invented), her big brother Finn, the odd sneaked glass of expensive red wine, all school food – especially pudding

Dislikes: Dresses, dressing up, poncy shoes and fussy clothes of any description, make up, fussing with her hair, fussing about anything at all, her real name

Would like to be: A professional rider – an international show-jumper, or maybe a three-day eventer – that way she could do show jumping, dressage and her favourite, cross-country jumping

Fascinating fact: She can be fully dressed in all her riding clothes and hat in twenty-five seconds flat

MIN

Full name: Asimina Singupta

Home: A big family house with a huge garden in a suburb of Durban, South Africa

Likes: Running really really fast and winning, being top of the class in every single subject, doing homework (it's so interesting when you really get into it), mango lassis, gold bracelets, reading science books, borrowing Amy's clothes, her Mum's home-made curries

Dislikes: The sight of blood, Biology lessons, baby-sitting her little brothers and sisters, the food at St J's, wearing her hair in plaits, Scottish grey skies

Would like to be: A medical researcher or medical physicist. She has to do something medical because of her doctor parents but it can't involve blood!

Fascinating fact: Min's mother taught herself Italian and went all the way to Pisa to get her medical degree

AMY

Full name: Amy Margaret McCorquodale

Home: An amazing penthouse flat in Glasgow, Scotland, with a terrace and panoramic view of the city

Likes: Designer jeans (Iceberg), designer bags (Marc Jacobs), designer boots (Jimmy Choo, but only when her Dad is feeling incredibly generous), Edinburgh's Harvey Nichols (obviously), very handsome boys, diamonds, champagne, dance music, dressing up and going out, her gran's mince and tatties

Dislikes: Penny Boswell-Hackett, Mrs Norah 'the Neb' Knebworth, everything in Niffy's wardrobe, French lessons, people teasing her about her Glaswegian accent, oh and Penny Boswell-Hackett (have you got that?)

Would like to be: Officially, she's going to do a law degree then join her dad's nightclub business. Secretly, she'd like to be a famous and fabulous actress

Fascinating fact: Amy's mum and dad were teenagers when she . . . er . . . arrived. She was brought up by her dad, her gran and her grandpa. She hasn't seen her real mum for years

Jealous Girl

Chapter One

'Gina, you can*not* go back there! You just can*not* leave us again!' Ria was lying back on a lilo in the pool, dangling a tanned arm into the cool turquoise-blue water. She was once again bringing up the subject which had bugged Gina all summer long.

'Ria . . .' Gina warned. 'I don't want to talk about this.'

'But Gina . . .' Paula began now, sitting up on the stripy sun lounger where she had been basting her lean black limbs in the shimmering heat of a Californian August.

'Yeah, Edinburro!' Maddison chipped in from the edge of the pool.

Gina, who was walking back out to the tiled pool terrace with a tray of iced drinks in her hands, felt as if she'd been ambushed. Had her best friends been talking about her? she wondered. Had they been planning this little debate while she was in the kitchen mixing up the tall cranberry and grapefruit coolers chinking with ice and soda water?

She knew why her friends were mad at her. Even though they'd all been together since junior high and she knew and loved all three of them very dearly, there were new friends in Gina's life now. There were reasons for Paula, Ria and Maddison to be jealous.

This wasn't about boys . . . well, OK, a certain boy with a wide, mischievous smile was maybe something to do with it. No, this was all because last term Gina had been dragged kicking and screaming by her totally fed up mother to a new school. Not just *any* new school either. Her mother's old school. Not in California either, or any other state in the whole of the US.

Gina, whose grades had plummeted, whose behaviour had apparently become 'unacceptable', whose all-consuming interest in clothes – and occasionally boys – was driving her mom wild, had practically been frogmarched onto a plane at LAX airport (though admittedly she'd been sent business class to ease the pain).

She'd been flown all the way to Scotland. To a grey, grey, chilly but beautiful city called Edinburgh. To a weirdly old-fashioned girls' school called St Jude's, which she'd pretty well hated for the entire first week at least. But then she'd started to make friends, and the friends were good ones; and then somehow it hadn't seemed so bad; and now, hadn't she promised her new friends, Amy, Niffy and Min – not to mention her mother – that she would definitely be going back in three days' time for the 'autumn' term and the Upper Fifth.

She might even (she and her mother were still in discussions on the subject) sit exams in Scotland next summer.

Gina approached the table, admiring her slim, brown, bikinied reflection in the huge glass doors that led to the terrace. Swimming every day, she'd gained sleek, toned muscles and a deep tan. Her hair had been lightened by both the sun and the expert attentions of her favourite colourist, Sandrina.

She set down the drinks and looked out over the pool. Long and deep enough to be really refreshing, it was picture-perfect blue. Ria's hand dangling in the water had set off ripple after ripple, causing the bright sunlight to dapple, wink and break across the surface.

Gina knew she was going to miss California. The daily bright, bright blue of the sky. The warmth that sank deep into your bones. And of course she'd miss these girls. All summer long they had been together: swimming, playing tennis, hanging out, shopping, driving to the beaches, catching up with other friends from her 'old' school. She couldn't quite get used to the idea that she really had left her Californian school; she kept telling herself that one day she might just come back . . . But Scotland and St Jude's was so different. It was hard to explain, but over there she felt like a different person. Here, she was surrounded by people who had known her for years and it seemed like nothing interesting ever happened. She knew what was coming next every moment of the day. But in Scotland it was as if she'd started afresh. Everything was new and she could invent a whole new future for herself.

'I'm going to really miss you,' she told her old school friends now as she went from one to the other, handing out the tangy sunset-red coolers.

'But you must be missing *them* more,' came Paula's grouchy reply as she took the drink, tucking her thick hair behind her ear.

'Well . . .' Gina began, wanting to explain.

'Yeah, your new Scottish friends are better than us,' Ria grumbled. 'And what about that cute guy?

You know, the one who's all over your cell phone.'

'Oh, yeah . . . well . . .' Gina tried to shrug it off.

'Yeah, well, nothing!' Ria teased. 'Have we all seen it, girls? Have we all seen the picture of little Mr Cuteness on Gina's cell phone?'

When the insistent shouts got too deafening and too embarrassing to tune out, Gina went over to her lounger and retrieved her cell from the shade underneath.

She called up one of the photos and her friends crowded round, all jostling for the closest look as she showed them the tiny shot of the boy who had given her an extra-special reason to return to Edinburgh at the end of the summer.

Dermot O'Hagan wasn't especially tall or especially handsome, but he was especially nice and he had a cheeky, friendly, downright disarming charm that made Gina smile, that made Gina relax, that made Gina feel just like herself – only better, because he clearly thought she was so great. It just shone out of his bright blue eyes and straight back at her that he thought she was *so great*.

During her first, difficult-to-adjust-to-it-all term at St Jude's, she had really needed someone who made her feel great. All the handsome boys from the other posh private schools hadn't been worth a second glance. But Dermot, who was sixteen and worked part-time in his dad's Edinburgh café, had turned out to be the guy who was just right for her.

He had been deliciously shy about asking her out – it had taken him weeks and weeks. In fact, he'd left it right until the last day she was in Scotland. So although they'd been emailing and phoning all vacation long, they'd only spent three whole hours together on an official date.

'So you're going back just for him?' Maddison asked, a smile on her face.

'No!' Gina insisted, but then she didn't say any more: she didn't want to hurt their feelings by talking about her new friends and how much she was looking forward to seeing them again.

'Going back for *him*? For him who?' Gina's mum, Lorelei Winkelmann was up on the wide balcony above them.

Wearing a blue and white striped summer dress and sunglasses, her hair swept back in the breeze, her arms stretched out on the railing in front of her, she looked like an old-fashioned movie star. Not that she was though. Lorelei worked in computing. She was a super-smart big-shot. Gina would always boast that

Lorelei and her partner, Mick, 'practically invented the Internet'.

'Gina, do you have a boyfriend in Edinburgh?' Lorelei asked with unmistakable disapproval. 'All summer long I've heard nothing about a boyfriend and now—'

'Grades, Mommy – I'm going back to Edinburgh to get good grades. Better than yours.' Gina looked up with a smile as she clicked her mobile shut.

She knew there was a weakness here. Her mother would not want Gina to go on about the lousy grades she herself had got when she was sixteen. Lorelei was a top business executive now: she drove a Mercedes convertible; she wore Armani. It would never ever do to admit to any past failures or weaknesses. These were things she had tried, unsuccessfully, to hide from her own daughter.

'Good grades! That's what you know I want to hear.' Lorelei smiled at her. 'OK, look out down there, I'm about to come and join you.'

But as soon as Lorelei stepped back inside the house, Gina's friends started up again:

'Don't go! Don't go back!'

'You can't leave us!'

'What about all the cute guys over here?'

'And the Halloween party!' Paula exclaimed in tones of total melodrama. 'You'll miss the Halloween party!'

Now this was true and kind of terrible. The Halloween party at Gina's Californian high school was a near legendary event. Costumes were planned months in advance; the entire hall and all the corridors leading up to it were elaborately decorated. The school paths and driveways were lit by no less than 150 intricately carved pumpkin lanterns. And there were loads of best costume prizes – although pets were no longer allowed.

'Tiber Flitberry isn't going to be allowed back in after what happened last year,' Ria reminded them.

'Oh yeah,' Maddison agreed, and they all cast their minds back to the screeches of horror when, from under his Dracula cloak, he'd released a real bat.

'What do you think they do for Halloween in Scotland?' Ria wondered.

'My aunt was in London last year,' Paula replied. 'She said they hardly do anything. The shop windows weren't even dressed up.'

'Scotland isn't exactly in London,' Gina reminded her with a roll of the eyes, 'but maybe I'll have to try and get them excited. Have a plan. Have a party even.'

She tried to imagine the imposing stone steps to the boarding house decorated with pumpkins, girls dressed up as witches and vampire victims, and boys . . . maybe they'd even be allowed to invite some boys?

'Do you realize, Gina' – Paula turned to her, and even the extra coatings of Clinique waterproof mascara couldn't hide the distress in her big brown eyes – 'we aren't going to see you again until Christmas!'

'Christmas? No way!' Ria and Maddison chimed in together.

'Well, there's only one thing you can do about that . . .' Gina began.

When her three friends turned to look at her expectantly, she told them, 'When my mum comes over to see me in November . . . you've got to come too!'

Chapter Two

Gina had plane hair. There was no other way to describe it. Her straight and usually well-behaved blonde locks were all frizzy and full of static.

Crammed into the tiny aeroplane toilet cubicle trying to apply concealer, then blusher, then lip gloss, while someone was rapping on the door and asking: 'Are you nearly finished?' was not exactly easy.

She pulled her hair up into a ponytail, but the more she fiddled with it, the frizzier it got. Pressing her lips together, she took one last look at her face. Despite the tan and the artful blonde highlights, she was hardly looking her best. No wonder – this was her eighteenth hour of international plane travel.

But when she stepped off this flight, she would be in Edinburgh, Scotland, local time 9.45 a.m. She glanced at her dainty silver watch: 9.23. Her stomach lurched with nerves because although it had been eight whole weeks since she last saw him, Dermot had promised he would be at the airport to meet her.

Gina didn't have to be back at the St Jude's boarding house until 4 p.m., so she and Dermot could spend almost the whole day together. Not that her mother knew anything about this of course. Her mother had been told that Gina would drop her bags at the boarding house early, then meet a *girl* friend for lunch, before heading back well before the four o'clock curfew.

When Gina and Dermot had planned their day together, on emails pinging their way back and forth across the Atlantic, it had sounded incredibly romantic and exciting. But now that Gina could hear the clunk of the undercarriage being lowered for landing, it felt . . . there was no other word for it: terrifying.

What would they *do* all day? What would they *talk* about? The plan was to go back to Dermot's house, so she could off-load her luggage and meet . . . his mom!

Gina thought there was a possibility that she might actually puke with fear. She checked in the seat pocket in front of her for a sick bag just in case.

'Welcome to *Edinburrrrrra*,' the air hostess announced with the soft Scottish burr that Gina had come to know during the summer term.

'Set your watches back ten years,' Gina muttered to herself. Because that was how it had felt the first time she'd arrived in Edinburgh from glittering all-new California. Like she had stepped back in time. Like she had boarded not just an aeroplane but a time machine that had taken her back to a place where everything was built of grey stone over a hundred years ago. Where people still wore tweed skirts and sensible shoes, minded their manners and used the mail to send letters. Where people, especially at St Jude's, talked about 'young ladies'. Where the 'young ladies' still wore ball gowns at least once a term and were expected to know how to do a formal Scottish dance.

It was weird, like a whole different world. Had she really liked it enough to come back? she wondered. Looking out of the window to see a steely grey-white sky above her and a drizzle of rain coating the glass, she wasn't so sure. Had she really wanted to come back to this? Maybe she'd just needed the adventure. Gina, who'd lived in the same neighbourhood since she was four, who'd had the same friends since for ever. Maybe Gina had needed something new and totally different.

But there was no denying that she was desperate to see her St Jude's friends again: Amy and Min. The other girl they had shared a dorm with last term, lovely, funny Niffy, was not coming back to school for a while but they had all promised to go and visit her.

And then there was Dermot . . . the lurch of nerves gripped her stomach again: of *course* she couldn't wait to see Dermot again. Could she?

As the plane came to a standstill, the FASTEN SEATBELT signs clicked off and the passengers began to stand up and collect their belongings together. Overhead lockers were opened and a scurry for bags and coats began, then the push and shove to get out onto the tarmac first.

Gina felt in her small but genuinely Prada handbag (a spoiling goodbye present from her mom) for her mobile phone. Opening it up, she registered the low battery warning and studied the photo of Dermot on the screen. She couldn't help smiling back at it. He was *lovely*! Of course it was going to be fantastic to see him again. Look at the way his long, sandy-coloured hair flopped into his face. She loved that. She loved the way he was always shyly pushing that forelock of hair out of his eyes.

Gina pulled her pink backpack down from the luggage compartment and joined the hustle for the door, then the long trek through the snaking corridors. She was walking quickly now, her legs just about keeping pace with her hammering heart.

Her fingers dipped into her back jeans pocket for her gloss and she coated her lips just one last time before fixing them into a smile. Then she pushed through the double doors and out into the arrivals hall.

As she cast a quick glance around the crowd, her first thought was: *Oh! He's not here yet!*

But then a boy stepped forward, waved and called out: 'Gina!'

She looked at him in bewilderment. It took an embarrassingly long moment before she recognized him. 'Dermot?' she asked hesitantly. He looked so different. A few photos on her mobile phone and a summer full of daydreams somehow hadn't prepared Gina for the reality of Dermot.

Here he was, standing, breathing, right in front of her, and she was suddenly so nervous she couldn't speak. He felt like a stranger.

His *hair*, for one thing! It was cropped close to his head. And he was in a scruffy red and green T-shirt and beaten-up jeans. She realized she'd only ever seen him in his café waiter's uniform of white or blue shirt, black trousers and apron.

'Gina!' he repeated with an infectious grin across his face.

'Hi,' Gina managed shyly.

Then he was enthusiastically wrapping his arms around her; he was moving in for a kiss!

She let his lips land on hers, but then pulled quickly back before he could get any more smoochy. Especially out here, in public. She felt as if he was someone totally new, rather than the boy she'd been emailing and texting all summer.

'You look great,' Dermot told her, keeping his arms wrapped around her waist.

'You look really . . . erm . . . different,' Gina replied.

'Yeah, that'll be my great tan,' Dermot answered with a grin, holding out a bare arm for her to view. It was as milky white as when she'd left Scotland in July.

'It's not been very sunny here then?' she asked.

'No. No, I don't think by Californian standards you could say that there has been much sun. No danger of any of us turning mahogany – unlike you, o sun goddess!' he teased. 'I take it you have heard of skin cancer and wrinkles and the hole in the ozone layer and all that . . . ?'

Now this was better. The Dermot Gina knew and had a phenomenal crush on was funny and teasing. This definitely sounded more like him.

'Yes thank you.' She slapped his arm playfully. 'So, your hair . . .' she began.

'I know, I know.' Dermot gave a satisfied smile. 'How cool and tough do I look? If I was in a film, you'd know I was the baddie.'

Gina made no reply; just looked at the haircut and the face, which was now so exposed. Dermot had alarmingly blue eyes and a wide, charming smile, but now that there was no bouncy forelock, his nose looked big and plain and his forehead seemed to protrude. The new hairstyle just didn't suit him at all.

'Uh-oh.' He seemed to sense that all was not well in Gina's gaze. 'You don't like it, do you? Oh no!' He smacked his palm into his forehead. 'Oh no! I'm going to get chucked because of my hair! She liked it better the other way. Oh no! It's all over!'

Although Gina had been tempted to blurt out, *Oh, you look weird! I don't know you!* before running away, now that Dermot was joking about his hair, now that he had voiced the problem and made fun of it, well, her reaction seemed completely ridiculous. His hair would grow. She would encourage him to grow it. In a few weeks he'd look just as cute as he had when she'd left for the States.

'I'll grow it out, OK?' Dermot was assuring her.

'I will grow my hair just for you . . . well . . . and my mum,' he admitted quietly. 'She doesn't like it either.'

'That's very kind of you.' Gina smiled back at him properly for the first time. Then she added, 'C'mon, I have to get my bags.'

When Gina heaved not just one but two enormous, bright pink bags from the airport conveyor belt, it was obvious that Dermot was a little taken aback by the quantity of luggage.

'Boy, these give a whole new meaning to the word holdall,' he joked, hauling the first bag onto a trolley and then struggling with the second. 'What have you got in here? A body you're trying to get rid of? No, no, don't tell me – this is one term's worth of haircare products, isn't it?'

'I'm not going home till Christmas,' Gina reminded him snippily. 'And I've brought back lots of presents, you know.'

'Presents?' Dermot, still in the act of manhandling the second huge pink sausage onto the trolley, sounded surprised. 'Presents? I didn't know there were going to be presents! Why wasn't I warned? Why did no one tell me? Why do I not seem to know any of the boyfriend rules? Is there a book about this that I should have read?'

'You've not got me a present then?' Gina teased, pretending to sound hurt but actually feeling a little shocked that he had used the 'boyfriend' word so casually.

'I am so chucked now, amn't I?' he asked.

'Totally,' she agreed, although her smile told him otherwise.

Moving closer, he put an arm round her and asked: 'Can we do that kissing thing again? Because I know I'd like to.'

Gina leaned in towards him, put her arms around his waist and tipped her face up slightly so that she could reach his lips. He pressed his mouth carefully down on top of hers and pulled her close. The weird tingle Gina remembered from kissing him the last time, before she went away for the summer, started up again. It seemed to travel from her lips directly to the pit of her stomach. A buzz, a flutter. She closed her eyes and kissed some more, opening her mouth just a little like Dermot had.

'Woo-hoo,' a little boy in a baseball cap shouted cheekily as he walked past them, causing Gina's eyes to blink open and the moment to pop like a bubble.

'Come home with me,' Dermot said a little huskily, not even turning his head to look at the kid; his hands slid into Gina's back pockets as he pulled her against him. 'Maybe we can do a little more of that. Provided my mum lets us out of her sight for longer than five seconds . . . Why, oh why did this have to be her day off?' He gave his forehead another theatrical slap, making Gina laugh.

'What's her job?' she asked, surprised that she'd never thought to find out before. She knew Dermot's dad ran the café where she and her friends hung out. This was how she'd met him – he worked there at weekends and school holidays to save up for his going-to-university fund.

'She's a midwife,' Dermot told her. 'Absolutely nuts about babies. Don't get her started. Please! You have been warned.'

'Gee . . .' Gina was impressed. 'That's such a *real* job.'

'Yes!' Dermot sounded amused. 'Very real. She works in a *real* hospital with *real* women, but unfortunately she doesn't get anything close to a *real* wage.'

Gina didn't say anything more, but she was thinking that being a midwife and running a café were both very different jobs to the kind of work her mom and stepdad did. Nowadays they were into licensing software or something. They didn't even design it; someone else did that. They were at the big money, selling end, Gina was sure.

Running a café or working as a midwife could surely never be as lucrative as licensing software. She knew Dermot went to an ordinary state school, so he wasn't like the private school pupils she'd met when she was in Edinburgh the last time – the privileged young ladies of St Jude's and the boys from Craigiefield and St Lennox, whose 'people' (parents) all seemed to live in four-storey Georgian townhouses, glamorous penthouses or large country mansions.

Gina knew that Dermot was from a different walk of life. And as he struggled with the trolley piled with her large pink bags, she realized that this was part of what was so interesting and exciting about him.

There hadn't been many 'ordinary' guys at her school in California either. Well . . . maybe there had, but she hadn't known them very well. Anyway, to live in that neighbourhood, your family had to be able to afford a home worth at least $600,000.

'These are going to be quite heavy to get onto the bus,' Dermot warned her as they headed for the exit.

'Bus!' Gina exclaimed. 'We can't take the bags on the bus! Is that how you got here?'

'Yeah,' Dermot answered. 'I had to get two buses. One from Craigmillar to the city centre, then the airport bus. That's what we'll have to do to get back to my place. I just wasn't expecting your bags to be so heavy.'

'We can't take a bus,' Gina said, standing there, refusing to take one step further in the direction of any bus. In California she never, ever took the bus. Buses were for poor people who didn't have cars; buses were dangerous.

'So what are you suggesting?' Dermot asked, palms turned up as if there were no other possible solution. 'There's no train,' he explained.

'A cab,' she told him firmly, astonished that he hadn't even thought of this.

'A cab? A *taxi*!' he spluttered. 'All the way to Craigmillar? Are you *mad*? That would cost a fortune.'

'Fine, I'll pay,' Gina told him. 'They're my bags, so my problem. My solution.'

'Gina, seriously,' Dermot warned her. 'It'll be about forty quid. Maybe even more.'

'That's fine, honestly.' Gina tried to reassure him, but now she seemed to have made him even more uncomfortable.

'But it's such a . . . such a waste of money.' Dermot made one final attempt to argue with her.

'Forget it,' she told him briskly, and strode ahead of him to the taxi rank.

There wasn't much chat in the cab. Dermot didn't seem to be able to take his eyes off the meter as it ticked steadily upwards, pound after pound. At every stage of the journey he asked the driver which way he planned to go, even recommending a different route – presumably in order to get to Craigmillar more quickly.

'The traffic's really bad that way,' the driver snapped back at him. 'I've just come from there.'

Gina looked out of the window because she didn't want to get involved in this discussion. The scenery was changing rapidly, from airport ring roads and dual carriageways to the solid stone houses that lined the roads towards the centre of Edinburgh. Passing the impressive grey buildings, Gina felt just as interested in looking at it all as the first time she'd arrived off the plane from LA.

It was so different! So grey, so elegant and so old. Just look at those black railings! All the houses so close together, the cars jammed nose to tail in every street. It was so very, *very* different from the lush modern buildings, huge gardens and gated driveways of her own corner of California.

And then they had passed through the town centre and were heading back out on the other side.

'We're going west,' Dermot told her. 'It'll be about fifteen minutes or so.' He gave the taxi meter another outraged glare.

They drove past scruffier blocks of flats in the more down-at-heel, studenty part of town, then the road opened out a bit and was now lined with small bungalows and pebble-dashed houses.

Gina had never seen this section of the city before. When she'd been at St Jude's last term, she'd either stayed at school or visited the town centre with her friends. There hadn't been any journeys further afield.

Now the taxi was turning off the main road and swinging through narrow side streets.

'How long have you lived round here?' Gina asked Dermot.

'About eight years,' Dermot replied. 'We used to have this great flat in Tollcross but my parents thought me and my brother should have a garden, be able to kick a ball around, ride our bikes . . .' He gave a roll of his eyes which told Gina that maybe he'd have been happier staying in Tollcross. 'I liked it round here when I was younger,' he added, 'but now it's boring.'

'You have a *brother*?' Gina asked him with some surprise. 'Why didn't I know that?'

'Malcolm? We keep him hidden in the attic – it's better that way,' he joked.

She dug her elbow into his ribs, glad to see him finally smile again. It was the first time since they'd got into the taxi.

'No, he's fine. He's just my little brother. You know how it is. You have one!'

And this was true: Gina had a half-brother called Menzie, who was about to turn nine. Of course she loved him; she missed him when she was away at school, but he also ... well, if she was totally honest, he could bug her to death.

'Am I going to meet Malcolm?' she asked.

'No! He's away with his football team for the whole day, so you're spared,' came Dermot's reply.

The taxi wound down a narrow road between yellow-brick houses with neat patches of lawn.

'The second left – it's number three,' Dermot was instructing the driver. The cab made the turn and immediately began to pull to a standstill.

Dermot turned to Gina; he sounded just a touch anxious as he said: 'And here we are. *Mi casa es tu casa.*'

'This is your house?' Gina's astonishment was obvious. But with just two windows on the ground floor, two on top and a small tiled porch over the front door, this was the tiniest house she had ever, ever seen. How did four people even fit in there?

Chapter Three

'Mum?' Dermot shouted out as soon as he'd opened the front door. 'I'm back . . . and Gina's here.'

For the next few minutes it felt a little awkward in the tiny hallway.

Dermot manhandled the pink bags in through the front door, where they seemed to expand and take up every available inch of space. Gina was crammed in behind Dermot, trying to close the door behind her. Dermot's mother was squeezing through in front of him, so desperate to meet Gina that she absolutely couldn't wait until they'd made it into the sitting room.

'Hello . . . hello there.' A woman who looked vaguely like Dermot but with curly red hair took Gina's proffered hand and pressed it between hers. She was chubby, smiley, with Dermot's kind blue eyes, but much shorter than Gina had imagined. Gina, in high-heeled new ankle boots, towered over her.

'Come away in,' Dermot's mum instructed her in that uniquely Scottish way. A not entirely friendly mix, it seemed to Gina, of 'go away' and 'come in'.

She was led by the hand into the sitting room, which was minuscule! The ceiling really wasn't very far from her head. But the room was bright white and almost bare it was so tidy, with a small leather sofa and two chairs facing an old-fashioned TV on a stand; a bookcase crammed full of hardbacks, paperbacks, periodicals and magazines lined one entire wall.

'Long journey?' Dermot's mum was asking her. 'By the way, you're to call me Jane. Shall I bring you some tea? You'll be needing a sandwich – something like that? I didn't expect you back so soon . . . I'm not quite ready. *You came by taxi?*' She looked at her son in surprise.

'No, *I* insisted on the taxi,' Gina said quickly. 'My treat. The bags were really heavy.' Surely that was going to be the last she heard about the clearly outrageous extravagance of a taxi?

'So, back to Scotland!' Jane began. 'I can't imagine why!' she added bluntly. 'Look at the weather out there – it's as grey as November. You leaving California and all that sunshine and your own pool! Just imagine!'

As Gina stood in this cramped room, glancing out of the window at the doll-sized, identical house on the other side of the road, gloomily lit by the greyish light, it seemed kind of crazy to her too.

'Dermot showed us all your holiday photos,' Jane went on; she was still standing, like Gina, who didn't want to sit without being offered a chair. 'Is that your house – the enormous white one with the pool? It looks wonderful. It must be like going on holiday, just going home. Does every house in California have a pool? Just like we all have lawns, do you all have pools?'

'Mum!' Dermot broke in. 'I think you'll find there are all kinds of people and all kinds of houses in California, just like anywhere else.'

'Is that right?'

'Well . . . yes,' Gina confirmed. Although, it occurred to her, she only knew people with pools. And that was probably a bad thing. One of the reasons why California was so boring to her.

'Tea? And sandwiches?' Jane asked again.

'Yes, fantastic, thanks. I've not had a cup of tea for eight whole weeks – but that would be perfect,' Gina replied.

'I suppose it's iced tea in California,' Jane said,

'to keep you cool. Bit of a different story over here.'

The tea and sandwiches were served at a small table, just big enough for four chairs, in the little dining room next to the cramped kitchenette. Gina had been in bigger trailers. Well, it was true, she had.

She couldn't help thinking of the kitchen in her home: a vast, shiny white and marble space, lit by the sunlight which streamed in through the huge windows. Her mom was only in there at the weekends though, because the rest of the time they had a *house-keeper*. Something she didn't think she'd ever want to mention to Dermot or his mum.

Dermot seemed so quiet – sheepish almost – while his mum went on about California and declared that if she lived there she certainly wouldn't be leaving to come to some school in Scotland.

'I suppose it is a very good school though, isn't it?' Jane asked her, but carried on without waiting for a reply. 'Your parents will be wanting you to do really well in your exams. Get some good Scottish qualifi-cations. Stand you in good stead when you finally go back home. So how long are you going to be here for?' She fixed her blue eyes on Gina.

'Gee . . . I'm not really sure . . .' Gina hesitated. 'I don't think we've really planned it out. I was supposed to come for a term, but then I kinda liked it, and now I'm maybe gonna stay for the whole school year and sit my S Grades . . . and after that . . . well, I guess we'll see.'

'So you'll have to make the most of her, Dermot,' Jane said to her son, which seemed to have a strange effect on him. He shrugged a bit, blushed a little, then choked slightly on his tea.

Once the mugs were empty and Gina had asked about Jane's job and listened to the baby rapture she had been warned about, Dermot interrupted and said he *had* to show her his new computer.

'I've finally got an upgrade. The old one was taking about ten minutes to download your photo files, so I've been on eBay, getting a sleek new – well, new to me – mean machine. C'mon,' he insisted.

Gina followed him up the narrow staircase and turned left. There was a bathroom at the top of the stairs, then a corridor with two doors ahead of them. Just two other rooms? Gina wondered to herself, incredulous.

She followed Dermot into the room on the left and found herself in a bedroom so filled with a bunk bed, a wardrobe and two desks that she had to stand close to him in order to fit in.

'Welcome to our room. Cosy, eh?' Dermot tried to sound cheerful, but the astonishment on Gina's face was obvious. 'I know, it's a bit titchy, isn't it? But it's funny how you get used to stuff. Our entire family is pathologically tidy – no bloody wonder: you'd only need to open a box of matches to cause complete chaos in here.'

And it was true: the room was gleamingly tidy and packed with ingenious storage. Under the bunk bed were large plastic boxes; at the end of the bed was a shelf stacked with DVDs and CDs and a tiny stereo system.

'My computer . . .' Dermot turned and began to tap at a keyboard on one of the small desks.

Compared to the shiny, silver, blinking, bleeping netbooks Gina's mom and stepdad carried about, this thing looked about a hundred years old. It was like Edinburgh: heavy, grey, solidly constructed and probably Georgian.

'Is that an antique?' she asked cheekily.

'Shut up!' Dermot said with a smile. 'Just because my parents don't work in the software business. We're not that poor, you know,' he added, eyes fixed on the screen. 'There's just a lot of money tied up in Dad's café.'

31

Gina was glad when he kept on looking at the screen, because she could feel herself blushing. She knew she wasn't supposed to notice how poor Dermot and his family seemed to be in comparison to hers, but the differences kept taking her by surprise.

Dermot fired the machine up, and with lots of whirring, wheezing and clunking, the screen finally came to life. Gina's blush deepened when she saw that his screensaver was a huge photo of herself in a bikini, holding a drink, with the bright blue of the pool behind her.

It all looked so bright, so vibrant and so totally at odds with this poky little room in the back of beyond that Gina felt a stab of homesickness pierce right through her; suddenly, just like Jane, she wondered what on earth she was doing here.

Then Dermot suddenly stood up, put his hands on her shoulders and brushed her cheek with his lips, reminding her that it wasn't all so bad.

'I think you should take a look at my photos,' he said.

'Your photos?' she wondered.

'Yeah.'

Gina looked about the room but couldn't see what he meant. Then Dermot directed her attention to the bottom bunk. All along the back wall were quirky shots and landscapes.

'Did you take those?' she asked, craning down to see.

'Yeah,' Dermot told her. 'It's OK, you can sit on the bed to get a closer look.'

'I can sit on your bed?' Gina asked with a teasing smile, feeling her stomach flip with excitement suddenly. She slid herself across the bed, propped her head up on her elbow and asked: 'Are you going to give me a guided tour?'

Not saying anything, not taking his eyes off her face for a moment, Dermot moved across the bed towards her. Then he was pressed in against her, warm, solid and excitingly unfamiliar. His hands were on the bare skin of her back and she was kissing him fiercely, feeling his breath against her face.

When she opened her eyes, she saw his dark lashes brushing against his cheek. She put her hand up to touch his face and was surprised by the prickliness of his jaw, but also by the softness of his cheek.

He was running a finger over the dip in her waist and it felt teasing and ticklish and—

'Maybe you two should go out! Show Gina the neighbourhood!' came Jane's shrill voice from the other side of the door, so loudly that they sprang apart in shock.

'Yeah . . .' Dermot cleared his throat. 'Good idea,' he added.

With a parting kiss on the tip of Gina's nose, he rolled off the bed and headed out of the door, telling her, 'I'll keep the dragon at bay – see you in a minute.'

Slowly, feeling almost dizzy, Gina got to her feet. She smoothed down her hair, fastened a blouse button that had come undone and looked around for a mirror.

Her eye fell on the computer screen. Dermot had left the documents list open and she scanned down it. Bio Proj 1, 2, 3 and 4 were listed; then came lots of photo files; then her eye fell on SCARLETT, a file name picked out in capitals.

Without even thinking about whether she should or not, she put her hand on the mouse and clicked the file open. Well, *Scarlett*? Could any girl have spotted a name like that on her boyfriend's computer and not have wondered who it referred to?

The file opened and Gina saw a page packed with typed words:

Lovely, lovely Scarlett, she read, *so smooth-skinned*

*and so kind, please just give me hope that one day you'll
be mine . . .*

'Gina?' Dermot called up from the hallway. 'How
about we go out for a bit?'

With an unsteady hand, Gina clicked the file shut,
tried to blank out the shock she was now feeling and
walked quickly out of the room.

In the weeks leading up to this date, this first proper
date with Dermot, Gina had imagined all sorts of little
scenes. She and Dermot in Edinburgh's beautiful
Prince's Street Gardens, licking ice creams and joking
together; she and Dermot running up the many stairs
to the very top of the Scott monument and kissing,
breathless, at the top; she and Dermot walking hand in
hand through the historic cobbled streets of the
Grassmarket . . .

Not one of her daydreams had included the tour
she and Dermot now took of this dull bit of suburban
Edinburgh.

Past a lacklustre row of shops, Dermot pointing out
his large glass-and-concrete high school in the
distance, then left into a graffiti'd play park.

When Dermot had said it was boring round here,
he hadn't been exaggerating. This was the most

boring place in boring land. Where *was* everyone for a start? Even though the sun had come out, the park was empty.

All the time, Gina was listening to Dermot talk and saying very little; she just wanted to shout out: *Who is Scarlett?* But she was too . . . too what exactly? Too nervous? Too scared? She was half-convinced that it was nothing – something she'd misread or mis-understood – but then she was also half sure that Scarlett must be the girl Dermot really wanted to be with but couldn't.

Dermot pushed his swing closer to hers, took hold of her swing chains and pulled her in towards him. 'Take me away from all this!' he said melodramatically. 'I can't believe I brought you out here! It was just because of the bags—'

'And because I wanted to come. I asked to see your home . . .' Gina reminded him.

'And now you've found out I live in a dog toilet and you're going to dump me. Please don't dump me!' he pleaded.

'Shut up, Dermot!' she insisted.

She liked him; she really *did* like him. But she felt all stirred up inside, and not just with the unspoken angst about Scarlett. Dermot was so different from her and all her friends. Without even mentioning it, he made her realize how rich her family and her friends' families were. Before, she'd never given it much thought; now she felt strangely uncomfortable about it.

Although Gina had dated a few boys from her school back home, that had just been like kissing school friends she'd known for ever. Getting to know someone new like this . . . It was so different, so nerve-racking. She didn't know yet if she could even commit to being with Dermot. All she could see ahead were complications: feeling jealous and confused about Scarlett, feeling too rich, feeling uncomfortable, feeling nervous and uncertain . . .

'Wel . . . it was fun while it lasted,' Dermot said with a teasing smile, his face right up close to hers.

She was looking deeply into his blue eyes, which were startling now that there was no curtain of hair for them to peep through.

Then his lips were touching hers again, and somehow when he kissed her and she closed her eyes, it was just Dermot, and everything was OK again. When he kissed her, Scarlett and swimming pools, teeny family houses and nerves didn't matter any more.

When Gina finally remembered to look at her

watch, she was panic-stricken to see that the time was 3.45! *What?* 3.45!

'Ohmigod!' she cried out, springing up from her swing. 'I have to go. I have to go right now – should have gone ages ago. I *have* to be back at the boarding house by four at the latest, or I am in so much trouble!'

Chapter Four

It didn't matter how quickly they'd run back to Dermot's house, how important they'd made it sound when they booked the cab or how speedily Gina had urged the driver to get there. When she pulled up at number 9 Bute Gardens it was 4.49. Late. *Late!* Being late was something they took very seriously at St Jude's. She shoved some notes towards the driver and hauled her pink bags out of the car as quickly as she could.

Already there were no longer any parents' cars in the driveway. The usual collection of estates, four-by-fours, glitzy saloons, BMWs and Mercs was all gone. To Gina's surprise, the only thing parked outside the imposing stone boarding house was a police car. What was going on?

She stumbled along as best she could, weighed down by the bags. Only a hundred metres to the front door, but then a set of stone steps ahead of her.

Gina yanked the bags up behind her, arms burning with the effort. She decided to take one first and then the other. She was just reaching the top of the steps with her second bag in tow when she looked through the big glass pane in the door.

Two women police officers in hats and thick bullet-proof vests, batons and cuffs hanging from their belts, were deep in conversation with the housemistress, Mrs Norah Knebworth.

Now, Mrs K may have been quite stout and quite short, even in her two-inch, block-heeled, shiny patent pumps, but she was formidable when her towering blonde beehive loomed up at you. Yes, somehow she did manage to loom *up* at people, in much the same way that taller, more frightening women could loom *down*. When she fixed her beady eyes on you and drew her lips into a thin line, crossed her arms underneath her terrifyingly solid bosoms, then yes, she was a force to be reckoned with.

There wasn't going to be any sneaking in late here, Gina realized. She was thinking fast . . . Could she say her plane was delayed? Could she say she met someone in town for lunch – an old family friend, or one of the school's day pupils – and plead that she'd lost track of time?

Maybe Mrs K, or the Neb, as everyone at the boarding house called her behind her back, would be too distracted by whatever was going on with the police to mind?

Anyway, what was going on with the police? People were only arriving back today. Maybe something had been stolen? Maybe there had been a break-in over the holidays?

Gina's hand was on the front door knob. Just as she began to turn it and push open the door, Mrs Knebworth's steely blue eyes swivelled away from the police officers and on to her. When they registered who was coming in through the door, dragging her bags behind her, she gave a screech of fury: 'Gina! *Gina Peterson!* I don't believe it! Where on earth have you been? Your mother called here to speak to you at midday. Everyone has been looking for you ever since then – we even called in the police!'

Oh, no! Surely not? Gina had expected a mild lecture for being forty-nine minutes late. She had not expected the launch of a full-scale police hunt. This was a *catastrophe*.

She swallowed hard. There were many sets of eyes

on her now: Mrs Knebworth's boring a hole through her, the two police officers' looking at her curiously, and several girls' who'd heard Mrs K's raised voice and had come into the hallway to investigate.

'Where have you *been*?' Mrs Knebworth demanded once again.

'Erm . . .' Gina hesitated.

The eyes continued to glare at her. 'I've been trying to call your mobile,' the Neb went on. 'Your mother's been trying to phone . . . We checked with the airlines that you had definitely arrived . . . Good grief, Gina, we were all beginning to think something terrible had happened!'

'I'm really sorry. My phone battery died . . . I thought my mom knew I was going to meet, er . . . erm . . .' *Stop hesitating!* Gina told herself. *Stop it or else she's going to know you're lying!* '. . . a friend,' she finished.

'No!' the Neb replied furiously. 'Your mother knew absolutely *nothing* about this! Officers' – she turned to the policewomen – 'I'd better let you go. As you can see, this case has resolved itself. I am so, so sorry to have wasted your time on this silly little girl.' Glare, glare.

Gina suddenly felt a hard lump begin to form in her throat. Here she was on the other side of the world with this old bat shouting at her already; no one welcoming her back. So she'd spent a few hours with Dermot and his mum – big deal! So she was fifty minutes late getting in the door? Even bigger deal! Why had she come back to this? Why was she not still in California with all the people who loved her so much?

The policewomen disappeared and Gina was left in the hallway to face the full fury of the Neb. The mouth, she noticed, had been pulled into a line, the arms were folded under the bosoms; it was going to be horrible.

Then someone rushed into the hallway at full tilt. A beautiful girl – tanned, with flying blonde hair, tight new jeans, multi-coloured silky top, jangling golden jewellery, smelling delicious and sparkly with glittery eye shadow and diamonds.

'*Gina!*' the girl shrieked with happiness. 'You're back!'

Then, regardless of Mrs K's stare, Mrs K's fury, Mrs K's looming lecture, Gina was caught up in a tight bear hug, with kisses landing on both of her cheeks.

'Grrrrrrrreat to see you again,' the girl said, rolling her 'r's as only a girl brought up on the west coast of Scotland can.

It was Amy. Oh! She'd totally missed Amy.

Chapter Five

'*Welcome back, Gina, you're gated!* This must be a new school record for the quickest ever gating. You didn't even make it out of the hallway and into the Neb's sitting room!' Amy, sitting cross-legged on her narrow school bed, was trying to make a joke of Gina's punishment.

The bed was littered with chocolate boxes and torn wrapping paper because the last twenty minutes had been a whirl of excited greetings, hugs and an exchange of the little presents and treats the girls had all brought back for each other.

Gina looked over at Amy, then across to her other friend, Min, before rolling her eyes. 'It's like I had lunch with the devil or something. I mean! His mum was with us practically the whole time. Eight weeks back home and I've forgotten what an alien species boys are supposed to be to St Jude's girls.'

Gina wrenched open the pink zip of her second bag and clothes began to spill out. First all the lovely new ones she'd bought while she was on holiday, which she was sure Amy would want to examine in detail; then the horrible St J's sludge-green uniform, which she'd had to put on for her friends back home, causing them to fall about with laughter.

'It's great to see you again,' she added, looking up at her room-mates with a big smile.

'Yeah!' Min agreed. 'The holidays seemed so long, but now we're back, it feels like only a few days since I last saw you. Strange!'

'It's just such a shame about Nif . . .' Amy tailed off. She didn't want to kill off the happy reunion mood in the dorm. She decided to change the subject. 'Why don't you tell us all about your date, Gina? Then all about your holidays, and then I'm going to tell you all about mine.'

'Yeah, well, don't hold your breath waiting for *my* news,' Min threw in. 'The all-Asian suburbs of Durban, South Africa, were not packed with adventure this summer.'

'You must be the only girl who comes back to school to have an exciting time,' Amy teased. 'Was it really that bad?'

Pretty, studious Min – real name Asimina Singupta – who was still wearing the green and gold sari she'd put on to wave goodbye to her large family at the airport many hours earlier, sat down on the end of her bed and began to play with her thick plait of hair.

'When I wasn't cooking or babysitting or visiting the numerous Singupta friends and relations, I had to do homework!' she told them.

'*No!*' Amy and Gina both chorused together. It was unthinkable that anyone should have to do homework during the summer holidays, and anyway, Min was easily the cleverest girl in their whole school year.

'The biology thing?' Gina asked. Both Min's parents were doctors and it was their dearest wish that their eldest daughter and all their other children should follow in the family footsteps. That's why she'd been sent all the way from Durban to St Jude's. The old-fashioned, long-established school worked its 450 day and boarding pupils hard and ensured that they all got the best possible exam results.

However, Min's weak spot was biology, mainly because she was so squeamish: just talking about a blood cell could make her feel faint.

'I thought that was all sorted out last term,' Amy chipped in. 'You're going to do physics and chemistry and specialize in medical research and radiotherapy and that kind of thing.'

'Yeah, but I'll still have to take biology right through school, so they want me to do well. They were just trying to help, I suppose. I got a letter from the Banshee during the holidays,' Min confided to her friends, 'and it wasn't exactly good news.'

'Uh-oh,' Amy sympathized.

The St J's headmistress, Banshee Bannerman – well, technically Mrs Patricia Bannerman – wasn't one of Amy's favourite people. It wasn't that there had been many run-ins. No, run-ins with the Banshee were a speciality of her other best friend and former dormmate, Niffy. As far as Amy was concerned, it was just a question of keeping a low profile wherever the Banshee was involved.

'You know how most of us are sitting nine S-grades this year, and some of us are doing ten? Well, looks like I'm going to be doing eleven.'

'Eleven!' Gina exclaimed. 'But that's crazy! You'll just be slaving away over your books the whole time.'

'Yeah,' Min agreed joylessly, 'but according to the Banshee's letter Miss Ballantyne was devastated to hear I wasn't doing history any more, so would I consider rejoining her class.'

'Boring!' Amy exclaimed. 'You know what this is all about, don't you? The great school league tables. You're bound to get an A in history, so that's one more A on the chart for the great St J's. God! I've had such a pure, dead, brilliant holiday!' She stretched out across her bed and kicked off her high-heeled boots. 'I have no idea why I've come back to this dump. My lovely dad says I can leave after Highers if I want to, so only two more years to go after this one!'

'Were you in the Gulf for the whole vacation?' Gina asked, admiring Amy's even golden tan.

'Dubai, Saudi and Egypt,' Amy replied. 'My dad quite fancied checking out the nightlife in Iran too, but I told him it wasn't going to be that interesting, what with all the burkas and no booze.'

'Is he thinking of opening up some clubs over there?' Gina asked.

'In Dubai, definitely. Everything else was just tourism and looking for new ideas. He's importing all these amazing Egyptian tiles to put in the toilets of his new club in Glasgow. All holiday I got to stay up till three or four in the morning with him. Then we'd get up late, swim in the hotel pool and do it all over again. I loved it!' Amy confided.

She was the cherished only child of a nightclub-owning multi-millionaire from Glasgow and her devoted dad was already keen to teach her all about his business.

'And what about Gary?' Gina wondered. 'Did he come with you?'

'No, Gary stayed at home . . . I don't know if all is well there,' Amy answered cautiously, 'but I'm keeping right out of it.'

It was only a few months since Amy's dad had come out . . . not just to her, but also to himself. There was no denying that her dad's *boyfriend* was an addition to her family that Amy was taking some time to adjust to. Before Gary, there had been just the two of them and, to be completely honest, Amy had preferred it that way.

As she turned her head to smile at Gina, the light bounced against her sparkling necklace and Gina exclaimed, 'Show me! Show me all your new jewels.'

With a little scream of excitement, Amy answered: 'Yes! One grand's worth of tax-free bling! I thought you were never going to ask!'

As Gina and Min crowded round her bed for a closer look, she took the dainty diamonds from her ears, undid her many gold and diamond bracelets and handed them over for inspection. Then, proudly, she unhooked her necklace.

It was a substantial gold pendant in the shape of a palm tree, worked in green and gold and studded with diamonds of different sizes, all winking and twinkling even in the light of the sixty-watt bulb hanging under a drab pink shade above their heads.

The St Jude's boarding house was so boring and unglamorous compared to the lives all three of these girls enjoyed back home: Amy lived in a huge white penthouse with jacuzzis, marble floors and a stunning view of the Glasgow city skyline; Min's family home was bright and showy compared to this shabby Victorian building which, although it had been repainted over the summer holidays, still looked worn and old-fashioned.

'Real diamonds?' Gina asked, running her fingers over the sparkling jewellery, although she didn't for a moment doubt it.

'Oh yeah, you'd better believe it, baby,' Amy confirmed, mimicking her friend's Californian twang.

'Will the Neb let you wear these around the boarding house? Will she even let you have them at school?' Min wondered.

'She will not be told,' Amy said. 'How's she to know they're all real?'

Just then the door burst open and a younger girl rushed into the room. Amy, Gina and Min looked at her in surprise.

'Amy!' the girl gushed. 'I just found out you'd been moved to the Iris dorm. I'm just down the corridor in Snowdrop, so we're neighbours!'

'Hi, Rosie . . . er . . . great!' Amy replied, but she didn't sound quite as enthusiastic about this. 'D'you know Rosie?' she asked, looking round at Gina and Min. 'She's in the year below us. Her dad was doing some work with my dad, so we were out in Dubai together and we . . . er . . . hung out.'

'It was *so* cool!' Rosie confirmed, and began to describe all the things she and Amy had done together. When she finally decided it was time to get back to her unpacking and left the room, Amy turned to Gina and Min.

'My new best friend,' she sighed.

'Well, isn't that a good thing?' Min asked her.

'She's nice,' Amy admitted, 'but I can't be as much of a friend to her here as I was when we were on holiday – I've got my own friends, and anyway, she's in the year below . . . You know, it's just not cool.'

'We could all do with a new friend or two now that Niffy is no longer here,' Min added, sounding irritatingly like a teacher.

Just the mention of Niffy's name was enough to bring a cloud of gloom over the dorm.

Niffy had been the other member of the dorm gang last year. No, she'd been more than the other member. She'd been a founding member, a lynch pin. This little dorm of just three beds seemed half-empty without Niffy's long, gangly frame and large personality. She and Amy had always shared dorms since they'd started at St Jude's as boarders when they were eleven. Min had joined them two years later, then Gina last term.

But now, for the foreseeable future, Niffy was living at home and attending a local school because her mother was ill.

'Did everyone hear from Niff in the holidays?' Amy asked.

'Yeah,' both Min and Gina answered. There had been emails, texts and even the odd phone call.

'She sounds OK,' Amy ventured, 'doesn't she? Anyway, she'll be in Edinburgh later this month for the Scottish hockey team trials.'

This news brought a groan from Min. 'Oh no! I'm supposed to be doing that as well. I'm never going to find time to do all this! I'll have to fluff it . . .'

'You're going to try and get into the Scottish hockey team?' Amy asked her. 'On top of your eleven GCSEs?'

'I know . . . can't be done, can it?'

'No!' Amy insisted.

'We're still going to visit Niffy on the first long weekend, aren't we?' Gina asked. She was totally intrigued by the prospect of visiting Niffy at her home – the one she'd heard so much about. Blacklough Hall, the ancestral pile, was apparently incredibly grand but falling down around its owners' ears. Gina also wanted to meet Niffy's beloved horse, Ginger, and all her dogs. Maybe they would see her big brother, Finn, as well. Yes, a trip to Blacklough was definitely going to be worth making.

'Yeah, of course we'll see her as much as we can. Poor old Nif,' Amy said, sounding slightly choked.

'She'll be back soon,' Gina soothed. 'I just know she will.'

Twirling her long blonde hair around her finger, Amy knew what would cheer everyone up: 'So . . . have I told you that I met Jason in the holidays?'

This reference to one of the most handsome but infuriatingly off-hand pupils at the boys' school,

St Lennox, brought mock screams from both Min and Gina.

'Jason!' Gina asked with wide eyes. 'Did you guys go on a date?'

Amy would only smile and nod, refusing all encouragement, threats or bribes to spill any of the details: the date had been so magical and so brilliant that telling anyone anything about it would just spoil it.

Gorgeous, dark-haired, impossible-to-pin-down *Jason* had actually travelled to Glasgow, her home town. They'd spent the afternoon in the city centre, visiting all the chicest shops and spending two whole hours just talking as they sipped drinks in the loveliest café. Then, holding hands all the way, they had gone back to the huge flat Amy shared with her dad, where Jason had been suitably impressed.

He'd admired the stunning view, the striking modern art and the designer furniture. He'd met her dad and totally taken in his stride how young he was and the fact that Gary was introduced as his boyfriend.

The moment he asked with gentle curiosity where Amy's mum was (to which the reply was: 'She had me at seventeen and gave me up to my teenage dad and his parents; I haven't seen her since'), he'd understood not to ask more. Maybe this was because he had a complicated family story himself, involving parents and step-parents across three different continents.

After dark, her dad had taken them in his chauffeur-driven Jaguar to his newest nightclub; they'd been ushered straight through to the VIP section, where they'd danced and schmoozed till two in the morning.

Jason had left on the train the next morning, after a late brunch out on the terrace. Both of them had drunk one half-strength cocktail too many to want to brave the rooftop jacuzzi.

Her dad hadn't exactly warmed to Jason, but as Amy pointed out, he needed to give him a chance and get to know him better.

That aside, the whole date had been wonderful – so it was an inexplicable, terrible shame that Amy hadn't heard a single word from Jason since.

Chapter Six

Gina, Min and Amy took their seats in the large wood-panelled assembly hall, where the names of former head girls and team captains were displayed in gold letters; they each carried a pencil and a little piece of paper.

At all the headmistress's big speeches – new term, end of term, leavers' day – they had always played Banshee Buzzword Bingo. It was Niffy's game, and today they were going to play it in her honour.

'If we didn't play it,' Amy had all but hissed, handing out the squares of paper, 'she'd be horrified.'

Unfortunately Amy had been spotted in the classroom minutes before as she was tearing up the paper squares.

'Missing your friend, are you? Playing her little game?' It was Penny Boswell-Hackett, the day girl who just had to have a go at Amy whenever she could. 'Poor little Amy – who are you going to snuggle up with at night now that your best dormie has left?'

'Shut up,' Amy had snarled back in fury. 'Just because you don't know what a best friend is – just because you probably have to pay those two to hang around with you . . .' She'd pointed at 'Piggy' and 'Weasel', the two girls who always tagged along with Penny.

'Bitch,' Penny had hissed back. 'Well, at least we've all got a chance of getting into the Scottish hockey team now that your overgrown clod of a friend is out of the way.'

'Wrong again!' Amy had been delighted to correct her. 'Niffy's travelling up especially for the trials. It turns out you don't have to be a snooty St Jude's girl to compete for the national team.'

'What's that round your neck?' Penny had flicked a casual finger at Amy's beautiful, prized necklace, which glinted from the open neck of her school blouse. 'Something tacky you picked up at the Barras?'

As the Barras was a well-known Glasgow street market, Amy was understandably furious. But her pithy reply had to be put on hold because just then their new form teacher walked in, called for silence, took the register, then marched her Upper Fifth B class down the corridor to assembly.

Walking along, Gina realized she'd forgotten how dark the school was. Even though the windows were big, they were set way up off the ground so you could only look out at the sky, which was a dull grey. In the corridors the floors were also dark grey, the walls greenish and panelled up to waist height in dark wood. Compared with life in California, it was like being underground.

After the school hymn, the Banshee took to the stage. She'd clearly had an invigorating holiday. Her stride, unhampered by her pleated skirt, seemed even more purposeful than usual. It was obvious that she must have been a lacrosse, hockey and tennis champion in her day. She would definitely have been team captain and head girl, her reports praising her 'leadership qualities'.

Gina glanced down at her list of words. Each time the Banshee said one of them during her speech, Gina would get ten points. '*Relish, challenge, address, smart,* and the bonus ball for a hundred points: *Santa.*'

She looked at the tall woman behind the podium, who swept back her short brown bob, gave a curt smile, took a breath and then launched into her sermon. There really wasn't a snowball's chance in hell that she was going to say 'Santa', was there?

After welcoming everyone back, telling her holiday anecdotes and announcing various staff changes, she added: 'Also, you'll be delighted to hear that there will be three Christmas balls at the end of this term: for Years Five and Six, Three and Four, Two and One. I'm afraid our younger girls will still have to make do with a visit from Santa. I hope that isn't too insulting.'

Amidst the polite tittering this brought, Gina was grinning: 100 bonus points! She put a big tick across her score sheet, while Min gave her a despairing glance and scrunched up her square of paper.

'I give up,' she whispered, earning herself a glare from Amy. Was she somehow insulting Niffy by doing this? she thought crossly. Niffy wasn't dead! Amy was going to have to lighten up about it!

Neither the tittering nor the paper scrunching was loud enough to drown out Penny's comment from behind them.

'Obviously the little cross around my neck is a family heirloom. It's Georgian. It's been in the Boswell-Hackett family for over a hundred and forty years. There are portraits of great-aunts of mine wearing it. Some people just haven't got any family history. Well, certainly not any that you could be proud of.'

This was clearly aimed at Amy. Min and Gina could

almost see her hackles rising. Gina put her arm on Amy's to restrain her and Min whispered a firm: 'Don't!'

But Amy, riled by the suggestion that she shouldn't be proud of her family, turned and hissed at Penny: 'Put your silly little bit of Georgian tat away! I'm wearing a grand's worth of Brand. New. Bling. Don't even *pretend* you're not jealous. Yeah, there are a total one point five carats in my new jewellery box – because *I'm* worth it!'

As the class filed out after the first assembly of term, Min couldn't help saying to Amy: 'Well, that's great. Let's just start the year off on a really good footing with Penny and her cronies. I don't suppose there's any hope that the great rivalry between you two is going to settle down or blow over?'

'Big. Fat. Chance,' Amy assured her.

Chapter Seven

'OK, I know this is not exactly fun, but there's no need to get vicious,' Gina said; Amy had just sprayed her with a shower of earth.

'I can't believe this!' Amy all but shrieked back. 'And it's not even a punishment! It's supposed to be some sort of hobby for us all. *Gardening?* We're fifteen! Not sixty-bloody-five!'

'Shut up, both of you, or it will just go on for longer.' Min had her head down and was hoeing steadily through the little patch of flower garden that had been assigned to the three of them.

The Neb – 'clearly menopausal', according to Amy – had decided that great improvements had to be made to the rather sad lawn, shrubs and patches of flower beds that surrounded the boarding house. The school's groundsman was clearly not up to the job, so she had decided to introduce the girls to 'the delights of gardening', as she'd put it in her dining-room announcement.

'Just an hour or two once a fortnight, that's all I'm asking of you – hardly more time than you currently spend doing the weekend washing up,' she insisted.

But there were unmistakable groans. The weekend washing up was bad enough, with its mercilessly strict rota which always seemed to throw up your turn unexpectedly and at the worst possible moment.

Tonight it was the turn of a small group of Upper Fifths to be handed hoes, rakes, spades – and orders to tidy up the flower beds.

'It's not just the gardening, is it?' Gina asked Amy – her friend had been in a barely disguised bad mood for days now.

'No, it's not!' Amy agreed angrily. Actually, hoeing wasn't so bad: it was a chance to take out some serious aggro on the earth.

'Jason . . . ?' Gina ventured. 'Still no news?'

'No!' Amy snapped. 'No news.'

It baffled her. They'd had such a good time! He'd told her it had been his best date ever – and *still* nothing! Had he lost her numbers? Should she text or email him with some reminders? No. In her heart of hearts she knew he had her details, because last term he'd done exactly the same thing: been out of touch for weeks, then suddenly reappeared to scoop her up and take her breath away.

And as for her dad's advice on the phone last night! She just wanted to forget all about it, but she couldn't get the lovingly meant words out of her head: *Amy, love, maybe he's just not that into you. Maybe you have to find someone better.*

Maybe he's just not that into you! Aaaaaargh!

'Unlike lovey-dovey, caring-sharing Dermot of course,' Amy couldn't help sneering. 'I saw you got another postcard from him today!'

'Yeah,' Gina confirmed, but she felt embarrassed. During the first fortnight of school, Dermot had emailed, Dermot had texted, and Dermot had now sent her two postcards.

The messages had begun cheerily enough: HOW ARE YOU? HOW'S SCHOOL? MISS ME YET? DOING ANYTHING AT THE WEEKEND? WANT TO SEE ME AGAIN? But because her answers had been so vague, he was now sounding a little sad and desperate. The postcard had read: *Gina? What did I do? At least give me a call. I'm sure we can sort this out. I'd love to see you this weekend.*

It didn't matter how nice and how keen he sounded, Gina only felt unsure. Did she *want* to get to know him really well? Who the hell was Scarlett? Should she ask him? And her newest anxiety: would Dermot one day treat her the way Jason was treating Amy? Gina never ever wanted to feel as miserable over a boy as Amy did.

She had tried before now to tell her friend how confused she felt about Dermot, although she'd kept her horrible anxiety about the Scarlett file to herself. But Amy hadn't been very sympathetic. He'd rung, hadn't he? Amy had pointed out. He'd emailed? He was desperate to see her again? What was her problem?

Tonight Gina was finally going to email Dermot: she was going to tell him that she just wanted to be friends. Yes. That was definitely what she was going to do.

'Hello, worker bees! Enjoying ourselves, are we?' The voice floated across the garden towards them.

'Just what we need!' Amy groaned.

They turned to watch Mel striding showily into the boarding-house gardens. Although it was mid-week, she wasn't wearing school uniform and looked as if she had been out somewhere interesting. Well, it was Mel's aim to make her life sound as interesting and colourful as she possibly could.

Unusually for a St Jude's girl, she had punk hair,

currently dyed the most vibrant shade of red she could get away with, eyes lavishly kohled in both black and iridescent green. The tightest black jeans, slouchy boots and a bright fuchsia jacket completed the look.

'Hi there, Amy! Gina!' she called out. Min was acknowledged with a nod because *she* was far too square to register on the Mel radar. 'We've not had a post-holiday catch-up.'

Standing around a flower bed was not the ideal spot, but clearly Mel – the self-styled boarding-house resident sexpert – couldn't wait to tell the three girls, each armed with a garden implement, all her news.

'Where've you been?' Amy wondered.

'At my delicious dentist's,' Mel giggled back.

'The dentist? What, Mr Rotherham?' Amy asked with a frown.

The man who scaled the boarding-house teeth and fitted the boarding-house braces was an excellent orthodontist but not exactly someone even *Mel* was likely to have a crush on. Mind you, there was no accounting for her taste. Last term she'd had a boyfriend called Bryan, and according to those who had seen him and reported back, he'd not had much in the looks department either.

'Pudgy, balding Mr Rotherham?' Amy had to ask.

'No, not Rotherham,' Mel told her with a dismissive wave. 'I go to a different surgery. Private. The guy responsible for the all-new Mel smile is gorgeous. But anyway' – she came closer and her voice dropped to confessional tones – 'I have a new man, and the most important thing you need to know about my summer is that I finally, thank God, lost . . . Do I need to spell it out?'

Well, no, she didn't.

All three sets of eyes were fixed on her expectantly. Mel was not exactly the kind of girl who held back with details, especially if those details were squishy.

But 'Phew, got that over with,' was all she said. 'I will be happy to fill you in, but at the right time and in the right place.'

This meant she had to be bribed in some way or other. She wasn't blatant enough to ask for money, but she might require a new lip gloss, a contraband cigarette or two. In fact, details as juicy as this might even require a half bottle of her favourite wine.

Amy scowled and carried on hoeing. The last thing she wanted to hear about was yet another happy couple. Anyway, she'd still barely forgiven Mel for having the nerve to snog Jason at a party last term, when she'd known perfectly well how Amy felt about him.

But there in the distance, coming out of the boarding house, was the one girl who might be able to help: Amy's brand-new best friend, Rosie.

'Hi!' she called out cheerily as she approached the group. 'Mrs K wanted me to warn you that she's coming out in a mo to inspect your handiwork.'

This provoked a round of universal groaning.

'Right, I'm off,' Mel told them, and turned towards the front door.

'As long as the Neb's not coming out to give us a hoeing demonstration,' Amy said. 'I do *not* want to see those monster bazookas boogie, not right in front of my nose.'

This reference to the Neb's ample cleavage made everyone giggle, and eyes were all fixed on the bouncing bazookas as the housemistress strode purposefully towards their patch.

'So what's going on here? Standing about gossiping like a bunch of old ladies! Get to work!' Picking up a spade for herself, Mrs Knebworth joined in, asking, 'What's the hot topic of conversation in Iris dorm this evening?'

'Halloween,' Gina said promptly, so they wouldn't have to stand around, guiltily silent.

'Oh yes, Halloween . . .' The Neb raised her eyebrows at Gina. 'Something of an American celebration, isn't it?'

'We should have a party!' Gina suggested. 'Something at the boarding house . . . something different!'

'A party?'

'We've had boarding-house parties before,' Amy pointed out. 'A DJ, some jugs of juice, low-alcohol lager and a handful of carefully selected nice young gentlemen.'

'Well, we have' – the Neb was now vigorously turning earth over, bending down grubbing among the roots of the weeds – 'but I'm never in any great hurry to repeat them. Things go awry . . .'

'But otherwise there won't be anything to look forward to until the Christmas Ball, and it's only September! More than three months to go!' Amy complained.

'We could carve pumpkins and serve blackcurrant juice and blue spaghetti and have fancy dress and prizes for the best costumes and it could be so much fun!' Gina went on enthusiastically, suddenly feeling quite desperate that the boarding house should have a party and a proper understanding of Halloween. Maybe she could even get her mom to send over Halloween paper cups and plates and pumpkin-carving stencils. You would be able to get pumpkins over here, wouldn't you?

'OK.' The Neb stood up straight and surveyed the work that had been done on the flower bed. 'Not looking too bad. You've definitely done your bit, girls. I'll have Year Four out here tomorrow evening – it's all coming along quite well.'

'The party?' Amy prompted her.

'Hmmm . . . What do you think, Min?' Mrs K's eyes travelled towards the quietest, most anti-social member of the dorm, maybe hoping Min would shake her head and the matter would be over.

'Well . . .' Min looked up and shrugged her shoulders. 'I think it might be fun.'

'See!' Gina and Amy both chorused together.

Once the housemistress had bustled back to the boarding house, issuing instructions about tidying away the tools, Rosie took Amy aside and insisted: 'I've got to talk to you about something . . . right away.'

Amy smiled because she realized all at once that Rosie was perfect. Rosie didn't have a boyfriend, Rosie had a long, long-standing crush on some boy who didn't even seem to know who she was, and Rosie was desperate to be her friend. So Rosie would listen . . . Rosie would definitely care . . . Rosie would maybe even have some advice for her about Jason.

Chapter Eight

Min, Amy and Gina set off from the boarding house early the following Saturday morning. It was a very important day: Min and Amy were going to try out for the Scottish junior hockey squad and, even more importantly, Niffy was coming up to Edinburgh for the trials as well.

Gina was coming along too: it was going to be the first time the four friends had got together since July, the end of Year Four.

'Niffy *is* OK, isn't she?' Min asked Amy anxiously as they reached the stop for the bus that would take them over to the sports ground at Meadowbank.

'Yeah,' said Amy, who had received an email from her the day before, 'but her mum's gone back into hospital, so Niff's coming up on her own by train for this.'

Both Min and Gina looked shocked at the news.

Niffy's mother was not well – she'd been diagnosed with leukaemia, a blood cancer. But Mrs N-B (as they called her) continued to cheerfully insist to both her friends and her family that it was 'the least serious type of cancer'; and anyway, 'they've caught it jolly early'. She was the type of woman who couldn't stand being ill and certainly wouldn't allow anyone to make a fuss.

'I don't know much about it,' Amy added. 'I don't know if it's anything unexpected or not. She's gone in for chemotherapy – maybe it's routine, just a normal part of the whole thing . . .' She tailed off because it was all too horrible to think about.

Once the girls arrived at Meadowbank, it didn't take long for them to find Niffy amongst the seventy or so hopeful hockey players already there.

She was rangy and seriously tall, with a luxurious head of brown, curly hair bundled into a messy pony-tail so that she could get on with the serious business of playing hockey. Niffy wasn't shy, so at the first sight of her dorm friends, she threw up her long arms and shrieked: 'There you are!' at the top of her voice.

'Hi!'

Ignoring the curious stares all around them, Min, Amy and Gina all ran over and took turns to kiss and hug her.

'I can't believe it's been so long!'

'Look at you! You're all so brown and beautiful!' Niffy was astonished.

'Should I take that as a compliment?' Min had to ask.

'Yes!'

'Look at *you*!' Amy interrupted. 'You're even taller!'

'I know, it's getting embarrassing.' Niffy waved her arms about in front of her long frame. 'You should see the size of Finn.' This was a reference to her older brother. 'He's already six foot four, and my dad says he's not allowed to drink any more milk because he's going to turn into a freak.'

The dorm girls already knew that Mr N-B was the kind of totally tactless parent who really would say something just like that.

'How are *you*?' Amy asked next, still holding onto Niffy's arm: she was so pleased to see her friend again it was hard to let go.

'I'm fine.' Niffy shot her a big smile. 'Really top form. And look at you, diamond-earring girl! You look gorgeous!'

'But what about your mum, Niffy? How is she doing?' Min asked sympathetically. 'What has she gone back into hospital for?'

'Just routine treatment,' Niffy replied. 'We're all very calm about it. She's just being amazing with all this boring stuff.'

'Boring?' Gina asked.

'Really boring.' Niffy rolled her eyes for effect. 'That's what she keeps telling me anyway. She's still in a total tizz that I'm not back at St Jude's – says I'm nuts to be going to Mill Park High. But, you know, I just wanted to make sure she's really OK ... before I come back.'

There was just a tiny little something about the way Niffy said this, some little hint of a choke to her voice, and her friends could immediately tell that under-neath the smiles and the shrugs, the 'boring' and the jokes, of course, deep down, Niffy was scared.

'But you're still going to come down to Blacklough and see me on the long weekend?' she asked.

'Of course!' all three friends assured her.

'C'mon!' she rallied them. 'You need to dump your bags and get ready!'

'I'll head up to the spectator stand,' Gina told them, but as she turned on her heel, she almost crashed straight into Penny Bosworth-Hackett.

'Oh! Hello,' Penny said coldly, taking all four of them in. 'A little dorm reunion, is it? I'd better not interrupt.'

She turned to go, but Niffy couldn't resist saying: 'Oh, get over yourself, Penny. If you get into this team, then we're all going to have to play on the same side for a change.'

'If *you* get in,' Penny snapped as she swivelled on her studded boot and stomped off.

'Just as lovely as ever then.' Niffy looked at Amy, knowing just how much she and Penny had always hated each other.

'Oh yeah!' Amy agreed. 'Let's try and smack her right across the shins if we get the chance.'

'But what if she *does* get in?' Niffy wondered. 'It'll be the first time she's ever played on my team!'

Niffy had every right to be confident that she would be selected. Her hockey, just like her lacrosse and her tennis – and any other sport she'd ever taken up – was incredibly good.

'Is there anyone here from your new school?' Min ventured.

This made Niffy cackle with laughter. 'No!' she answered. 'If there was a junior Scottish chip-eating team though, they'd be fighting to join.'

This comment startled Amy. She'd been born and brought up in the East End of Glasgow, and had lived there until the age of eleven, when she'd been sent to

St Jude's. A lot of the friends she'd had in primary school weren't exactly sporty, but they were as hard as nails – if that was the kind of school Niffy was at now, she wouldn't be finding it easy to fit in.

Among the crowd of girls at Meadowbank today to try out for the under-seventeen team, a practised observer could spot that while not every girl was from a private school, they were definitely in the majority. How would the observer tell? There was just something about the long flicky hairstyles, the posher voices, the expensive uniform tracksuits and woollen jumpers.

The girls too could tell their own kind at a glance. It was a tribal thing: each could recognize her own.

Gina sat in the third row of the stand and watched. Several coaches with clipboards blew their whistles, calling the girls to line up and divide into groups.

'We're going to play you in teams,' one of them began to explain. 'Those of you happiest in attack stand to the left, those of you who like to defend to the right please. Now, hands up, goalies – you are going to be trialled by the two captains of last year's under-eighteens.

'OK, play your best – the girls who are likely to really impress us are the ones who play as a team and who save goals and score goals,' she finished.

After a quick selection process, there was another shrill blast of the whistle and the first two teams headed over to the pitch closest to Gina. At first she couldn't spot anyone she knew in either of them, but then Niffy was called on to play.

Brimful of confidence, her short skirt and hair flying, she began by charging up, then down the field, determined to get her share of the action. *If you want action, you've got to be action* was just one of Niffy's on-field mottos.

To Niffy's delight, Penny was then called as centre forward on the opposing team.

'Just like old times then,' Niffy warned her cheerfully as soon as she was within earshot.

The girls fought each other for the ball. Up and down the pitch they went, other players trailing in their wake. Then, as Gina watched from the stands, she saw Penny break away with the ball; then, *horror!* she had scored!

'Excellent! Nice goal,' the coach enthused. With a blast of her whistle she signalled for some substitutes to come onto the pitch, and out came Min.

Before Niffy could even register how pleased she was to see her old team-mate back, Penny had charged in, tackled Min and passed the ball on to another forward.

'Bumarama!' was Niffy's furious response to this. She shot off, hard on Penny's heels, but it was no good – the ball was passed back to Penny, and within seconds she had deftly scored again!

The coach blew her whistle and, to Gina and Niffy's dismay, Min was taken off.

'You only get one chance to impress out here!' Penny sneered.

Now Gina could see Amy's blonde head bobbing towards the pitch. *Ha!* she couldn't help thinking. *That* would show Penny! Niffy and Amy both working against her.

But to Amy's obvious astonishment, she was put in Penny's team!

'I'm not playing with *you*, I'm playing for a place on the team!' Penny snapped at her.

'Yeah, I think that's kind of obvious,' Amy snapped straight back.

'Just make sure you keep out of my way,' Penny warned.

The whistle blew and Gina couldn't take her eyes off the match. What would happen now? she wondered.

Penny and Niffy seemed to be fighting it out at every turn. A spectator could almost have forgotten there were twenty other players on the pitch, eager for a share of the play.

Now Niffy had the ball. *Finally!* Gina thought, a smile spreading across her face as she watched her friend sprint along at full speed, the ball totally under control at the tip of her stick. Finally she was going to get a chance to prove herself!

But no! One of the defenders rushed forward, took the ball from her and fired it up the pitch, where it found Amy.

'Pass,' Penny hissed at her.

Amy understood her options perfectly: pass to Penny and she risked watching her score for the third time. Then Penny would definitely be picked for the Scottish team. Amy, who'd made her look so good, might even be picked too. Wouldn't that be a laugh? Training sessions with Penny, matches with Penny, away games and long foreign trips . . . with Penny.

No. No way. Absolutely *no way*! Never, ever. It was *Niffy* who should be picked for the national team. She was really, really good. She deserved a place. And anyway, if Nif was on the team, she'd be up in Edinburgh regularly for practices and Amy would get to see her much more often.

That was all Amy wanted: to see plenty of Niffy. She'd thought she needed to be on the team to do this, but now she saw that so long as Niff was on the team, it would be fine.

'Pass, you airhead!' Penny hissed across the pitch, and at these words Amy suddenly found it easy to deliberately fumble the ball and send off a wonky shot that landed exactly where someone on Niffy's team would get it.

Just three fast passes later and Niffy had scored. She celebrated her victory by running straight up to Amy and giving her a high-five.

'Totally pathetic,' Penny fired at Amy, once she'd made sure the coach was out of earshot.

It was not until ninety minutes later that the coaches had whittled down their selection by playing the group of hopefuls in a series of brutal matches, and the Scottish under-seventeen squads were announced.

'Penny Boswell-Hackett' was read out, and there was a long wait as the coach went alphabetically down the list before announcing, 'Luella Nairn-Bassett.'

'Yessssss!' Niffy and Amy weren't shy in shouting out their excited response to this.

It wasn't a guaranteed place in the Scottish team for either of them, but a place on the thirty-strong squad.

'Nice try, losers.' Penny's comment was aimed mainly at Amy.

Amy turned her back on Penny and pretended she hadn't heard a thing. 'When's your train home?' she asked Niffy.

'No hurry. I thought we'd all go to the Arts Café for old times' sake.'

No one had told her about the ongoing awkwardness between Gina and Dermot then . . .

'You could go and see your dishy lover boy,' Niffy bumbled on, quite unaware of the glances Amy and Min were shooting at Gina.

'Ha!' was the first thing Gina said.

'Oh dear – has it all gone wrong?' Niffy asked. 'Nobody tells me anything!'

'Oh . . . you know, not really . . .' Gina began. But inside, she was deciding not to be a baby. In fact, she was going to be big about this. Wasn't she? She'd been to the guy's house, she'd eaten lunch, met his mum. She couldn't go on just ignoring him. Could she?

'No,' she insisted, tucking her little Prada up underneath her arm, 'it's fine. Honestly, let's just go. I'll be fine.'

'Have you told him you might see him this weekend?' Amy wondered.

'Well, not exactly. Erm . . . vin fact, no. I told him I just wanted to be friends.'

'Oh . . .' Niffy, Amy and Min all replied together, finally understanding exactly how awkward this was going to be.

Chapter Nine

Saturday afternoon on a beautiful September day and the café wasn't too crowded because people were out and about – shopping and strolling around and enjoying the very last burst of summer sunshine.

As soon as the girls came in, they were spotted by Dermot, who was working his usual Saturday shift. Because he was pale-skinned, his vibrant pink blush didn't exactly go unnoticed.

'There's a big table free – over there in the corner,' Min pointed out helpfully.

Gina gave Dermot a smile and a wave, then followed her friends over to the table.

He stood very still and seemed at a loss – unsure whether to smile and wave back, or turn on his heel, or glare . . . or what? He settled for running a hand through his hair with a confused look on his face.

As soon as Gina and her friends had settled down

in their chairs, he approached them with his notepad at the ready.

'Well, hello there,' he began, his clear blue eyes meeting Gina's. 'This is a bit . . . unexpected.'

'Hi, Dermot.' She gave him a friendly smile back. 'How's it going?'

'Oh . . . I'm fine. Nice of you to ask,' he added pointedly. 'What have you been up to?'

'Well' – Gina was finding his gaze unsettling; she was now fiddling with her hair a little nervously – 'I've been busy at school . . . and Niffy's come up to see us. She's just been picked to play in the Scottish hockey team.' She hoped this would move the conversation on.

'Hey! Well done. That's great.' Dermot turned and offered Niffy his outstretched hand to congratulate her.

As he and Niffy shook, Gina took a proper look at him. He was in his café uniform: blue shirt, black trousers, blue and white striped apron. His hair had grown out just a little since she'd last seen him. Watching him hold Niffy's hand and smile warmly at her, Gina couldn't deny the pang she felt. But she still thought it was best if they were just friends. Friends was fine. Then she wouldn't need to feel jealous or anxious, or suffer any kind of pain when he went off with Scarlett . . . or whoever else.

'How's your mum?' Dermot asked Niffy.

'She's doing really well,' she told him, her voice resolutely cheerful – although she was just beginning to realize, sitting here in the café with her three friends, that she would give anything to be back at St Jude's with them and for life to be back to normal. She was deeply jealous of their wonderfully normal lives.

'So you've left the Daffodils?' Dermot asked her. Last term the four had shared the Daffodil dorm at the boarding house.

'She has, but only temporarily,' Amy chipped in. 'And we're not Daffodils any more.'

'No, we're Irises,' Min told him. Although she was generally shy around boys, she felt at ease with Dermot because he was so nice and friendly to them all.

'Oh, Irises . . . Much more classy.' He treated her to one of his kindest smiles. 'And how are *you* doing?' he asked her. 'They've managed to drag you away from your books for the afternoon?'

'Yeah . . . but apparently you're a bookworm too,' Min replied, remembering some of the details of Gina's date.

'Oh!' Dermot seemed almost flustered. 'Did

Gina tell you that?' He nodded in her direction.

'Yes,' Min went on. 'She said your house was full of books, that you've read most of them and you're one of the smartest boys she's ever met.'

'Hmmm.' Dermot was colouring up a little at this. 'Did she say anything about me being cute though? Funny? No? Devilishly handsome? Because if it was all just about how clever I am, then I'm in big trouble.' He risked giving Gina a teasing smile.

But she was starting up with a fierce blush of her own. This was just too cheeky. Why was he asking Min to reveal her secrets?

Luckily, before Min had to try and come up with the tactful and diplomatic answer that these questions demanded, there was a sharp: 'Dermot! The orders!' from the gruff-looking man behind the counter.

Dermot gave him a smile and a quick salute in response.

'Is that your dad?' Gina asked in a low voice.

'Yup, the one and only. I'd introduce you, but he's in a very grumpy mood, and anyway, I'm not quite sure where we are . . .' He gave her a very frank, direct look, which made her heart beat nervously. 'Friends . . . ?' he asked, keeping his eyes on hers. 'More than friends . . . ? You know what? I'll leave you to think about it. So . . .' He straightened up and looked down at his notebook, pencil at the ready. 'Don't tell me, double skinny latte, no sugar, no chocolate on top.'

'Yes,' Gina answered. Here at least was one question she could cope with. 'Thanks.' She smiled as nicely as she could, to make up for the fact that she really didn't know how to answer his other questions yet.

When Dermot returned to the girls' table with their coffees, he was annoyed to see that three guys he recognized from the snooty Edinburgh boys' school St Lennox were settling down beside the four Daffodils – no, Irises; he wasn't going to be able to get that into his head. They'd always be the Daffodils to him. One of the guys was even squeezing himself into the small sofa right next to Gina!

'So lovely to see you!' Charlie Fotheringham's loud, posh voice was booming across the table. 'Tell me all your news! Niffy! Why are you here? I thought you were on a leave of absence.'

As the dorm girls took turns to explain all the latest to him and his two friends, Dermot set the mugs down noisily on the table, then grumpily took the boys' orders.

'I had a brilliant summer.' Charlie settled back in the sofa, his arms behind his head.

Amy and Min were exchanging annoyed glances. Neither of them had actually invited the boys to sit down at their table like this. They were both desperate to hear Niffy's news and find out how she was settling in to her new school. As for Gina, she just wanted to be left alone to think about Dermot properly, logically, without this nervous hammering in her chest. None of the girls were really in the mood for flirty chat from these three boys.

But never mind – Charlie was clearly intent on telling them about the fun he and his pals had had waterskiing off the Cap d'Antibes all summer. Aha – that was why they all looked so good: deep brown tans; hair tousled and lightened in a way that could only be achieved by a long hot summer in the Med. They sported the expensive casual clothes that marked them out as the wealthiest of the wealthy St Lennox boys: preppy Gant and Ralph Lauren labels, shiny leather belts and beautifully cut jackets – one of them even had a Tag Heuer watch glinting softly on his wrist.

Dermot, who was hovering behind Gina, tried to be subtle. He leaned down over the back of the sofa, brushing against her arm and hair, and whispered to her, 'I'm not working tomorrow . . . Would you like to meet up in the afternoon, my *friend*? I want to go and see an exhibition at the Modern Art Gallery, and they have fantastic cakes. Almost as good as here,' he added persuasively.

At his accidental touch, Gina felt a shiver travel down the back of her neck. Suddenly she thought of them kissing on his bed, and the burst of warmth in the pit of her stomach fired up once again. But still, she didn't want to commit to something as definite as another date with him. So she told him, 'I'll call you, OK?'

When Charlie heard her utter these words, he turned his head in astonishment, saw her talking to Dermot and boomed out, 'Gina, are you dating the waiter? The *waiter*?'

'Why don't you mind your own business?' Gina told him calmly.

'But,' he spluttered, 'St Jude's girls don't go about dating the – the hired help.'

Could he have sounded more snobbish?

'*What?*' Amy exclaimed. 'Welcome to the twenty-first century, Charlie. Shame you missed the twentieth!'

'Nice guys,' muttered Dermot under his breath,

just loud enough for them all to hear. But he didn't want to cause any sort of scene, especially with his dad already in such a bad mood, so he turned on his heel and walked quickly away.

'Charlie, you pompous arse,' Niffy said gently, with a teasing smile yet quiet authority. And at this, Charlie bit his lip.

This was Niffy's power. She had a big brother, so she was totally at ease with boys in a way that Gina, Amy and Min just weren't. But more than that: pompous, titled members of the Edinburgh aristocracy didn't overawe her because her mum had been to school in Edinburgh; her grandmother and even her great-grandmother had been to school in Edinburgh. She knew these people. She had been to their christenings, their toddler birthday parties; she knew all their parents; she even had a stately home of her own. She was one of them in a way that Amy, Gina and Min were not, never would be and would never *want* to be.

So when Niffy called Charlie a *pompous arse*, he had to listen.

'Well, she's only a Yank,' Charlie muttered. 'What can you expect?'

At this, Gina felt angry tears spring to her eyes;

more than anything else she wanted to hit Charlie. But, like Dermot, she didn't want to make a scene in his café.

'Charlie, I think it's time for you and your friends to buzz off,' Amy said between gritted teeth. 'You see, we only have Niffy for another hour or two and we'd like to keep her to ourselves.'

Gina caught Min's eye. Min was looking at her over the top of her cappuccino.

'Do you think Dermot's OK?' she asked Gina in her quiet, clear voice.

That was all Gina needed. Before the boys had even picked up their coffees, she was already on her feet. She'd decided to tell Dermot that a date at the Modern Art Gallery tomorrow would be fine – would be *more* than fine, would be *great. Delightful.* She was glad that Charlie was such an idiot, and that Min was so thoughtful – because together they'd helped her to see quite clearly what a very nice boy she had on her hands in Dermot.

She caught up with him at the counter, where he was loading a tray with an order for another table.

'Do you still want to go out tomorrow, Dermot?' she asked quickly, before he made her too nervous to say the words. 'Because I know I'd really like to,' she added, to make sure that he understood why she was there.

But Dermot turned to her with a serious face. 'You know what?' he began, picking up the tray and turning away from her. 'It's obvious we don't belong together, so I think we should just forget it.'

Chapter Ten

A note, folded so often and so tightly that it looked like a little ball of paper, plopped onto the classroom table in front of Amy. She looked round but couldn't immediately see where it had come from. There were seventeen girls in the English class, all with their heads bent down over the afternoon's assignment – a comprehension test based on some half-page of writing so long-winded and tedious you had to wonder why the examiner had bothered with the ten ridiculous questions. The first one set the tone for the rest: 'When the narrator uses the word "derogatory", what do you think he means?'

Amy had been writing, but with all the enthusiasm of someone trying to stave off sleep. She'd even felt her eyelids sagging once or twice, so the small note ping-ing onto her table was an excitement, to say the least.

Gina had seen it land too; even Min had been

roused from her frantic scribbling to give it a quick glance, but then she'd sniffed and made a disapproving face. She didn't like any distractions from her work.

'Go on,' Gina urged under her breath. 'Take a peek.'

Amy moved the ball of paper down out of sight onto her lap, then quickly unfurled it.

The scribbled words in front of her read:

Suzie Woodrow's lawyer dad has been charged with drink driving but it won't be coming up in court because he's done a deal. Pass it on.

Amy glanced up at Suzie, who was sitting at the table across from theirs. She had paused for a moment in her writing and was chewing the skin at the corner of her nail while looking distractedly out of the window.

Someone else might have taken this as proof that this little titbit of gossip was true, but Amy wasn't impressed. She wasn't impressed by the gossip either. This was the kind of titbit you got when you were in a classroom full of Edinburgh lawyers' and doctors' daughters. It almost made her homesick for her old school, where the hot chitchat was, as often as not, about whose dad had gone to jail. In Amy's book, if you couldn't get off a stupid little drink-drive charge, what was the point in being a flaming lawyer?

She picked up her pen and wrote at the bottom of the note:

You call this gossip? Penny B-H having nits is much more exciting than that. Pass it on.

Then, making sure that Mrs Parker's head was bent over her desk, she flicked it idly onto the table Suzie was sitting at, just to stir things up a little.

'Girls!' Mrs Parker raised her head, suddenly filled with fresh enthusiasm for the lesson. 'I haven't told you about the house competition we've come up with here in the English department.'

Some barely suppressed groans met this announcement.

Amy was one of the groaners: hadn't Mrs Parker and her inter-house competition caused quite enough trouble last term when Amy had stood against Penny in the debating contest? Yes, Amy's side had in fact won, but only by the skin of their teeth, and it had been one of the most terrifying experiences of her life to date. No way was she going to repeat that. Whatever

Mrs Parker was going to suggest, Amy was not going to get involved. No. Definitely not.

'Obviously the summer debating season is over' – Mrs Parker pushed back her frizzy blonde hair and shot Amy, then Penny, a significant look – 'and a lot of fun it was too,' she added. 'And there was I thinking that blood sports had been banned . . . No, no, this term . . .' She stood up and walked in front of her desk, revealing to the class her sassy purple and black dress with matching waistcoat in all its glory.

'Where do you think she shops?' Gina hissed into Amy's ear.

'eBay,' came Amy's tart response. 'It's either eBay or India, or maybe Monsoon. All equally bad.'

'Girls!' Mrs Parker shushed them. 'This term we want to inspire you to get involved with the dramatic arts . . .' The English teacher seemed to enjoy the slight hush that this announcement brought. Although most of the girls in the room realized that their career options were limited to doctor, lawyer or accountant, a few still nursed a secret longing to be Hollywood film stars.

'We want those girls who are interested to submit a one-act play. The four most fascinating *oeuvres* will be performed, one by each house. I'll be holding open auditions to choose the cast and the directors. Fun, no?'

Despite her promise to stay out of it, Amy felt her ears prick up. Acting? Yes, obviously she was going to join her dad's nightclub business after she'd done a law or business degree, but she was one of those girls who couldn't help daydreaming about acting just a little. Maybe having a famous actress on board wouldn't be such a bad thing for her dad's business anyway . . . would it?

'A one-act play?' Penny was the first to start with the questions. She was already taking notes, eager to get cracking. She was just such a prize-hunter, already doing everything she could to make sure she was appointed head girl in two years' time. 'So how many words are you looking for?' was her next question. 'How long should it take to perform?'

Mrs Parker was more than happy to elaborate, and provided a list of recommended plays as 'inspiration' for all those planning on entering the competition.

Amy, Gina and Min wrote down the suggested titles.

'Interested?' Min asked Amy.

'Not writing . . . but maybe acting. Gina?'

'Erm . . . yeah, I think so,' Gina answered casually, but really she felt excited. She was definitely going to give this a go. Her one really good subject, the one she felt totally comfortable with, was English. Or, more accurately, English with Mrs Parker.

And anyway, Gina's most secret ambition, which she had never told anyone about, was to be a screen-writer – so yes, she had to at least give Mrs Parker's one-act play competition her best shot.

'I hope you're not even thinking about writing a play on top of your heavy workload?' Amy had to ask Min.

'Well . . . I—'

But before Min could reply, Mrs Parker's voice cut across them: 'Giselle, could you bring the ball of paper that has just landed in front of you over to me?'

When Giselle stared up blankly, pretending to have no idea what she could possibly mean, the teacher wasn't fooled.

'Yes, that little ball of paper right there – the one that's just landed on your notebook.'

Giselle paused, then her hand went gingerly to the rolled-up ball. 'I haven't read it, Mrs Parker,' she said meekly.

'No? Good. Well, just give it to me.'

'Uh-oh. This is going to be interesting,' Amy whispered just loudly enough for both Gina and Min to hear.

Chapter Eleven

Amy had woken the following Saturday to see the yellow curtains over the dorm windows glowing with early morning sunshine. As soon as her eyes were open, Jason was the first thought that came into her mind. She'd finally heard from him yesterday. He'd sent an email to say he wouldn't be able to meet her in town today (her suggestion, her emailed invitation – God, she could just kill herself for being so stupid as to invite him out again; how *desperate* did she want to seem?).

I'm a bit tied up for school all day Sat, he'd informed her in his reply. *Sunday no better, but I'll let you know ASAP if next weekend might work. J.*

J? *J?* This was someone who had held her very tightly in the darkest, cosiest corner of the nightclub and kissed and kissed and kissed her until she didn't think she would be able to breathe again. Until the only thing she could see, smell or think was Jason. In that corner, on the plush velvet sofa, set back from the throng, out of her dad's sight, Amy had practised snogging.

She had finally begun to understand what all the fuss was about as she'd let Jason's mouth fix over hers and his hands pull her tightly towards her. Together, they had felt the surge of want. Big, breathless, fearless want. Kissing Jason, she'd felt as if nothing else mattered, not one single other thing in the entire world. When she'd kissed Jason then, she'd felt as if she'd have gone anywhere with him and done any-thing he wanted to do. She'd been aware of what a heady and slightly dangerous feeling it was.

But that was six weeks ago. Since then nothing but long silences, brief texts, and now this email turning down a meeting and not telling her when another one might be on the cards. Amy could just scream with frustration. What was the matter with him? Hadn't they had a brilliant time? The best time ever?

No, she wasn't going to let this carry on any longer. Today she was hatching a plan: she was going to find out what was really going on with Jason. What was he really up to today?

Straight after breakfast, as soon as the girls were allowed out of the boarding house, she planned to set off for St Lennox's. She didn't know what excuse she was going to give. It was difficult to leave the boarding house on your own. But maybe she could say she had to buy more uniform and would meet up with her friends later, before they all returned to the boarding house for lunch.

Amy dressed carefully: if she was going to spy on Jason, she couldn't wear anything too eye-catching, but then, if there was just the slightest chance of him seeing her, she couldn't look *too* bad. So she chose jeans, a black top, her very soft, very expensive copper-brown leather jacket and, for a little touch of colour that wouldn't announce her presence, her high-heeled red ankle boots.

She brushed out her hair carefully and applied blusher, lip gloss and perfume.

'Is there something we should know about happening today?' Min asked, her head emerging from the casual sweatshirt she was pulling on. 'I thought this was a quiet and boring weekend before the big trip to Blacklough next Friday.'

'Next Friday?' Gina double-checked. 'That is *so* exciting!' The prospect of visiting Niffy in her weird ancestral home in the wilds of the countryside was definitely thrilling.

'I will explain it all later. Once I know exactly what is going on,' Amy told them both, not taking her eyes off her reflection in the mirror. 'All I need you to do is cover for me – just for a few hours.'

'Uh-oh,' said Gina, who was still in bed – she hated getting up so early at weekends (at St Jude's a lie-in was something that went all the way to 8.30!). 'Why do I get the feeling this has something to do with racey-Jasey?'

'Don't call him that!' Amy snapped. 'And I'm not saying anything until later. All I need is for you two to go into town for a few hours this morning, then we'll meet up, maybe a little later than I'll be telling the Neb, and come back to the boarding house together.'

Both Gina and Min sighed, but it was clear from the determined look on Amy's face that this was the plan.

'Are you going off to meet him?' Min wanted to know.

'Not exactly,' was all Amy would say.

As soon as she'd signed herself out, convincing Mrs K that she was in dire need of a new games skirt and she'd be hooking up with her friends within the hour,

Amy almost ran down Bute Gardens. At boarding school, being on your own was so unusual that when it happened, it gave an almost delirious sense of freedom.

At the end of the street she took a right then a left turn, which brought her onto one of the busy roads leading into town. She wasn't going to town, but within a few minutes she had spotted what she was looking for: a taxi with its light on, ready to pick up a fare.

Hailing it and jumping into the back, Amy instructed, 'St Lennox School on Macmillan Road please, but don't drop me right outside the gates.'

Once she'd paid the fare and watched the cab rattle off into the distance, she wasn't so sure about her plan. The big, imposing gothic building took up almost the whole street. Yes, there was one main front entrance, but she couldn't just stand there hoping Jason would suddenly appear. What *was* she thinking? There were probably loads of different side gates in and out of the place. And anyway, there was nowhere to hang about unnoticed. She couldn't exactly crouch down behind this row of parked cars . . . could she?

It was quiet though – no boys were coming or going out of the place yet. Maybe they had assembly on

Saturdays . . . or church? Or even classes? She couldn't remember if any St Lennox boys had ever told her what happened on Saturday mornings.

Standing all alone in the road, looking at the deserted gates, the deserted driveway up to the school, she felt overwhelmed by the task she'd set herself. How was she even supposed to *find* Jason, let alone spy on him?

Disheartened, she turned away and began to trudge towards the road that led into town. Walking up the steep hill, she passed a little café and decided to go in, order a coffee and just think about the whole thing for a few minutes.

When she was seated with her creamy latte at the table beside the window, she suddenly realized that, quite by chance, she'd ended up in a prime position. Wasn't this the most obvious route for St Lennox boys to take into town? If Jason was up to something far more interesting that meeting her, wasn't this the way he would come? And if he *didn't* walk past here, couldn't she at least think about believing that maybe he really *was* tied up at school for the day?

She sipped her coffee and watched and waited.

Time passed.

Then time began to drag.

Soon time was absolutely crawling along from one minute to the next.

Amy had felt a rush of excitement when the first group of St Lennox boys – not in school uniform, but nevertheless completely obvious because of their off-duty gear of slim jeans, suede boots and cord jackets – had sauntered past, laughing and joking. But now she'd probably watched as many as ten groups like this go along the street – and still not a hint of Jason; not even anyone she recognized from Jason's year.

This was pointless and hopeless. Checking her watch, she could see that she had wasted well over an hour of her life on this completely daft idea.

What would her dad say to her if he knew about this: *Stop kidding yourself! He's not worth it!*

Right. She would finish off her third cup of coffee and give up. Whatever Jason was doing today, she wasn't going to find out about it.

She set down her coffee cup, picked up her dainty little designer handbag and stood up, but then what she saw on the other side of the window made her shrink back down into her seat. There, only a metre away from her, she was sure she'd seen him! He was walking quickly, on his own, but she'd recognized two distinct features: the swish of his dark hair and the light camel suede jacket he'd worn when she'd met him at Queen Street station in Glasgow.

She was *sure* it was him. Fumbling with notes and coins in her purse, she paid her bill and then went carefully out of the café door.

Scanning the pavement ahead of her, she just caught sight of the suede jacket as it rounded a corner and turned left. She ran up the hill to catch him and soon found herself following Jason at a distance of about thirty metres.

She'd never done this before – it was terrifying. Her heart was thudding in her chest and she wondered what on earth she would do if he turned round: just one glance and he would surely know it was her. Obviously she'd have to make some excuse about why she was here in this part of town on her own... Visiting a day girl – that's what she'd tell him.

Anyway, he was the one who ought to be feeling awkward if he saw her! What was he doing walking into town when he'd said he would be tied up at school all day?

Amy tried to block from her mind the thought that Jason must be meeting another girl. But it kept coming back to nag at her. He was on his own; he was really nicely turned out... Where was he going?

It was a steep, steep climb up the hilly streets towards the centre of town. Jason was walking very fast and Amy almost had to jog to keep up with him. Clearly, private detectives must wear trainers so they'd be able to run after suspects and sneak about quietly.

Jason turned into George Street, which was busy with Saturday shoppers. For several moments Amy thought she had lost him in the crowd, but then she saw his dark head resurface like a seal's popping up in the water. At least she was concealed by the crowd too, but she now had to stay much closer so as not to lose him.

All of a sudden he made an abrupt right turn into Café K. Amy stopped in her tracks. She didn't know what to do now. He was obviously meeting someone, but she couldn't go in and subtly spy on him from inside – he would see her. So what was she supposed to do? Just hang about outside?

As if by some miracle, her phone began to ring. Mrs Knebworth had agreed that as the dorm girls were meeting up in town, they would be allowed to take their mobile phones out with them. A rare treat. Mobiles were usually kept in a locked cupboard in the boarding house.

OK, at least Amy had a reason to stand still. She was

on the phone, phoning . . . thinking hard about the call — so hard that she had to stay put, but with the phone against her ear she wouldn't look like a total idiot just standing there in the middle of the pavement.

'What time are you going to meet us?' she heard Gina's voice asking her. 'We've been up and down Prince's Street, up and down George Street . . . We're a bit bored now.'

'Ummm . . . something's come up. Major development. Can't come now,' Amy told her in a whisper, though she wasn't sure why — it wasn't as if Jason could hear her, now that he was probably shmoozed up to some new girl in the cosiness of Café K.

'Go to the Arts Café,' Amy suggested. 'Chill out with Dermot and I'll be along in an hour or so.'

'I don't think so!' There was an angry edge to Gina's voice.

Amy didn't have time to discuss whether or not Gina should make up with Dermot or get over him — all the pros and cons and the ins and outs — because right then Jason, holding a takeaway coffee cup, stepped out of Café K.

'Gotta go,' she told Gina and cut the call off abruptly.

If Amy was surprised before, she was now even more astonished to see a graceful, golden blonde gazelle of a girl spot him, stop in her tracks on the pavement, lean towards him and kiss him on both cheeks.

Look at her! She was beautiful and glamorous, and so swishily, elegantly dressed in her pristine black Uggs and her slouchy green cashmere wrap thing. Oh, good grief! This had to be the living, breathing, glamorously highlighted proof that Jason had a date!

Jason and the gazelle smiled at each other and chatted. Amy could feel a great big crack forming in her heart: she was tempted to break cover, leap out and scream at him right here and right now. But then the cheek kissing broke out again – and the gazelle went one way and Jason began his purposeful striding in the other direction.

What? *Really?* She was just a *friend*? They had just been chatting? She'd only bumped into him by accident! All at once Amy could have skipped, hopped and danced right up to Jason and planted a few choice smackers of her own.

But he was walking off so quickly, not even breaking stride to sip at his coffee. She was almost jogging in her attempt to keep up – at a sensible distance of course.

Down onto Prince's Street they went. Jason didn't bother waiting for the lights, he just scooted through moving traffic in a daredevil way which Amy had to copy just to keep him within sight.

Now he was marching towards the really steep hill of The Mound. Where was he going? she wondered. Up at the top was the Royal Mile: tourist central – hundreds of shops selling cashmere, crystal and tartan tins of shortbread. Yes, there were flats, cafés, restaurants, museums and university buildings as well, but why would he want to come here? This was a part of town she and her friends rarely ventured into.

Amy was beginning to pant. Her heart was thudding because she'd drunk too much coffee and done far too little exercise during the school holidays. A bit of swimming and disco dancing was hardly the same as all the dashing up and down hockey pitches and around tennis courts, not to mention the miles of cross-town walking she was used to during term time. The eight-week holiday had left her out of condition.

Unlike Jason, who'd obviously spent the summer cross-country running or something.

To get to the top of The Mound, there was a vicious flight of old Georgian steps built of solid grey stone;

Amy knew he was going to hit those any moment now and she would have to follow on behind.

As soon as Jason reached the Playfair Steps, he began to run up them! She watched in despair. After all this effort she was in serious danger of losing him, just as he was getting to wherever he was going. Amy's phone began to ring again, but seeing that it was Gina, she quickly switched it off. Then, taking a deep breath, she hurried up the steps as quickly as she could, heart pounding, breath rasping, deeply, deeply regretting all four of the cigarettes she'd smoked during the holidays. (God, if her dad found out he'd kill her. He had nothing but contempt for smokers: 'Sad losers. Addicts. Filthy coughers.' He didn't like to employ people who smoked and had even decorated several of his nightclub's outdoor smoking areas with skulls and crossbones.)

Amy had her head down, concentrating on every step – surely not many more to go now? she thought. She glanced up, sure she would see Jason's figure way out ahead on the road above. But there was no one there. Oh no! She was *way* too slow! He'd already made it round the corner: unless she speeded up, she wouldn't be able to get up there in time to see which way he'd gone.

Making a final, gasping effort to accelerate, head down, she stumbled up the last of the steps, clinging to the cold metal railing. To her surprise, she crashed straight into someone – someone tall and lean – but the first thing she felt was the velvety softness of suede.

Too stunned to register it, to do anything other than hang her mouth open like a goldfish, she looked up and saw that she had run straight into Jason.

He was facing her and he was grinning – had he doubled back down the steps? she wondered. Then the thought struck her: had he been *waiting* for her?

'Hello there, Detective Inspector McCorquodale. I had no idea I was so interesting,' were Jason's words of greeting.

Amy could feel a blush rampaging up her face, so she hung her head and found herself looking at his shoes. Scruffy green and white baseball boots. Cool. He was always cool.

'Hello,' he said, as if beginning again. 'It's really nice to see you . . . I think.'

Then he wrapped his arms around her and she felt her head being pulled in against suede shoulders, and suddenly she thought she might cry. This was just too much. He was such a confusion! And so confusing!

'Where are you going?' was the first thing Amy blurted out.

'Why are you so interested?' Jason asked, but there was something of a laugh in his voice.

'Where are you going?' she repeated, pulling away and staring at him angrily.

'I need a new pair of rugby boots for my match this afternoon.'

'And you can get those on the Royal Mile?' she asked, unconvinced.

'No. Just off George Street,' he replied. 'There's a sports shop there.'

'So why are you up here?' she demanded.

A lazy smile crossed Jason's face. 'Wel . . . I spotted you coming up the hill behind me and then waiting for me to come out of Café K. When you didn't say hello, but just hid round the corner, I thought I'd—'

'You've run me all the way up this hill for a laugh?' Amy was furious with him now. Flustered and red in the face, she didn't care what he thought of her, the stupid twit. She stamped her foot at him, swivelled on her red heel and began to stomp down the steps again.

'Hang on!' Jason called out and began to follow her down. 'I think it's funny! I think it's very sweet of you.'

This just made Amy speed up to get away from him.

Now she was blinking tears away, head down, hands balled into fists, not wanting him to see how upset she was because of him.

'Amy!' he called out after her. 'I'm sorry about today. I'm busy all afternoon with the match and I don't have a late pass from school. I couldn't get out today.'

'You're out!' she stormed at him. 'Couldn't we have had a coffee? Just for an hour this morning?'

'Well, yeah,' he answered. 'But I didn't think you'd want to do that. I wanted to take you on a proper date and show you the kind of fantastic time you showed me in Glasgow.'

This stopped Amy in her tracks. *A fantastic time in Glasgow?* So he still remembered it as a fantastic time?

'Where have you been since then?' She turned and stormed at him: 'No phone calls? No emails? You couldn't even send me a flaming text. Unless I contact you first, you never think of me for a second!'

'I do,' Jason told her, and his face seemed to cloud over. 'I've been . . . tied up.'

'Yeah, tied up! Like you're tied up today! If it's so fantastic when we get together, why don't you want to get together more?'

He reached out and put a hand on her shoulder.

'Stop it,' he urged. 'You're here now, I'm here. Do you want to come and buy some rugby boots with me? Then, I don't know . . . We could get an ice cream.'

An ice cream? Did he think he was her uncle or something?

'An *ice cream*?' she blurted out in dismay.

'Yeah, I love ice cream,' Jason said with his most persuasive smile.

To her surprise, she found herself laughing, and then they were laughing together. To her further surprise, Jason caught hold of her hand and kissed it, as if he were some debonair prince or an old-fashioned film star.

She felt the brush of his upper lip against her fingers so intensely it was as if time had slowed down for those few seconds. Then they walked hand in hand to the sports shop. Afterwards, Jason bought them both a ninety-nine cone from a van by the gardens alongside Prince's Street. Then, still hand in hand, they walked all the way back to St Lennox, where Amy had to say goodbye because Jason had a rugby match. He *promised* – he absolutely one hundred per cent *guaranteed* that he would call and they would arrange to do something together next weekend.

Only when he was well and truly out of sight did

Amy think to glance at her wrist watch. It quite clearly showed that the time was 1.15! *Mince!* How had it got to 1.15? She was supposed to have signed in at the boarding house fifteen minutes ago, and worse, much worse, she knew that Gina and Min would already be there. But what would they have told the Neb?

Chapter Twelve

As Amy sprinted up Bute Gardens towards the boarding house – the amount of running around she'd done this morning was going to kill her – she tried to listen to the garbled messages on her mobile. Yes, her *mobile*! The one she'd forgotten to turn back on after her little tantrum up on The Mound.

An increasingly frantic Gina and then Min had raged at her voicemail: '*That's it, we're going back. We can't hang about hoping you'll call or we'll somehow bump into you. We're taking the bus. We'll get off at the usual stop and walk back very slowly. Hopefully we'll meet you on the way.*'

Well, that had been quite nice of them, Amy had to admit. She was going to have to think of an excuse though. She tried to remember all the advice Niffy – a totally expert liar – had ever given her. Keep it simple. Keep it casual. Never over-elaborate. Just go for the obvious. *Expect to be believed!* That had been her mantra. *Expect to be believed.*

Amy opened the door of the boarding house and saw at once that lunch was over. She might as well go straight into the Neb's sitting room and see if the dragon was there – she wanted to get this over with as soon as possible. She knew she was in real danger of being gated next weekend. Burning at the forefront of her mind was the devastating possibility of *missing* her date with Jason.

'Mrs Knebworth?' she said meekly, poking her head round the sitting-room door.

The housemistress was ensconced in her favourite armchair with her feet up, her reading glasses perched on the end of her nose and one of the Saturday newspapers spread out on her lap. Hearing her name, she swivelled her steel-blue eyes in Amy's direction, then narrowed them at the sight of her.

'You are forty-five minutes late,' her tirade began, 'and you very obviously did *not* meet up with your friends as you promised me you would. This is completely unacceptable, Amy. I will *not* have girls roaming about Edinburgh on their own. It is against the house rules—'

'Mrs Knebworth,' Amy interrupted before the

terrible words 'you are gated' could be issued. She knew that once they had been said, they could never ever be taken back. The Neb would never tolerate any challenge to her authority. She would rather gate the innocent by mistake than retract a gating. 'I am so, *so* sorry,' Amy began, because nothing less than full-on grovelling was going to get her out of this. 'The uniform shop didn't have any skirts in my size, so they sent me over to the branch right on the other side of town . . .' Amy was straining her memory . . . *where* was that other shop again?

'And did *they* have the skirt?' Mrs Knebworth had now put down the paper and was peering at Amy over the top of her glasses, her eyebrows raised.

'No . . .' Amy had to say that, because otherwise, why didn't she have a shopping bag with her? 'They sold the last two in my size ten minutes before I got there,' she managed.

This was too elaborate, she realized at once – Niffy would have thought of something better. Much more simple and clever. She was tangling herself up in knots.

'I tried to meet up with Gina and Min, but . . .' Amy went on, moving away from the skirt. But *what*? She couldn't do a mobile-flat-battery story because that could be checked; and she couldn't say she'd entered both her friends' numbers incorrectly because that wasn't likely . . . 'But the signal was really weak out there.'

'How curious – weak signal in Morningside, and all those mobile phone users out there.' Mrs Knebworth made a tut-tutting sound.

'So then I decided to come straight back and there wasn't a bus for ages.'

'You should have taken a taxi,' Mrs Knebworth commanded. Her gaze was still fixed on Amy.

Amy had no idea whether she was succeeding here or not. Did Mrs Knebworth believe a word she was saying?

'If I'd seen a taxi all the time I was waiting at the bus stop, I'd have taken it,' she said meekly.

'Oh, the bus service is frightful as soon as you're out of the city centre,' the housemistress agreed; to Amy's surprise she looked almost sympathetic.

And that's when Amy remembered that the Neb didn't drive and had ranted about terrible local bus services in the past.

'I couldn't believe it,' she hazarded. 'I was just waiting and waiting and waiting. According to the timetable there should have been a bus every twelve minutes.'

'Oh, I know,' Mrs Knebworth agreed. 'It's absolutely ridiculous. And like you say, no taxis ever pass that way, so you're stuck.'

'Totally.' Amy nodded vigorously.

'Well . . .' Mrs Knebworth looked at Amy searchingly, as if making one last attempt to sniff out a rat. 'These things happen,' she said finally.

Just as soon as she could get out of Mrs K's sight, Amy hurried off in search of Gina and Min. She found them in the Upper Fifth sitting room.

'Did you see him?' was Gina's first question as soon as Amy came in.

'Yeah!' And despite the tension of the last thirty minutes, just thinking about her mini-date with Jason brought an unmistakably dreamy expression to Amy's face. Much to the amusement of her friends.

'Oh boy, oh boy! So how did it go?' Gina was desperate to know.

But their conversation was interrupted by a knock at the sitting-room door and Amy's friend Rosie from the year below poked her head round.

'Hi, Amy!' Rosie enthused. 'Can I come in? I saw you going in here and I'm just desperate to know how it went. Did you see him? What did he say? Are you guys going on a date soon?'

As she came into the room, firing questions at Amy, Gina felt her irritation growing. She just didn't like this girl knowing even more about her friend than she did. And it certainly didn't escape her notice that Rosie was wearing exactly the same jeans and an almost identical top as Amy. How could Amy stand it?

'It was great!' Amy gushed. 'We're definitely going to meet up next weekend.'

'Oh, you *are* smitten,' Min giggled. 'He's even made you forget that we're going to Niffy's next weekend!'

'Nooooooooooooooooooooo!'

Chapter Thirteen

The Friday evening train journey from Edinburgh to Berwick-upon-Tweed wasn't a long one, but as they approached their destination, the weather grew worse and worse. The cloud and gloom deepened, then fierce rain began to lash against the train windows.

'Remind me again why we are going to spend the weekend in the countryside?' Amy said, looking out at the current view of jagged black rocks and swirling sea. 'There's absolutely nothing to do out there.'

'We're going to see Niffy,' Min reminded her. '*She*'ll keep us entertained!'

'You're just in a grump about your Jason date,' Gina told her.

'Hmmmph.' Amy continued to stare out of the window. She'd already tried to reschedule the date for the following weekend, but Jason wasn't sure if he was playing rugby or not.

'What about Sunday?' she had asked on the phone, trying to keep the pleading tone out of her voice.

'Yeah . . . we'll see. I'll call you,' was all she'd got out of him.

When Gina saw how upset Amy was about Jason, she tried to feel glad that she and Dermot were now so over. He hadn't called or tried to contact her once since that day in the café. *Just as well*, Gina told herself. *He's probably with Scarlett now! And good luck to them.* She tried hard to ignore the sharp little jab of pain this thought caused her.

Scarlett. Scarlett . . . Whoever Scarlett was, Gina couldn't stop herself from imagining how gorgeous and witty and bright and bubbly she must be – compared to her. Ha. Maybe Gina would centre her one-act play around the mysterious Scarlett, and maybe she'd come to a horrible end . . .

'So are you really prepared for Niffy's home?' Min asked her, and although Gina nodded, Min nevertheless began to tell her once again about the horrors of Blacklough.

It was dark and still raining when the train pulled into Berwick-upon-Tweed station.

Amy hauled her overnight bag down from the luggage rack with the words: 'Here we are! Brace yourself for the full country-house weekend experience.' Then she rolled her eyes at Gina just to underline that it might not be quite what she was expecting.

But after Min's latest warnings, Gina felt very well prepared – she felt *over*-prepared; in fact she wished she'd been spared a few of the more grisly details: the horrible food, the arguing parents, the huge dogs that hung their heavy heads in your lap and drooled on you at dinner time. Min was particularly anxious about the dogs.

'Still,' Amy said as they headed towards the door, 'we get to see Nif for a whole weekend; we get to find out how she's really getting on. It's worth putting up with the rest of it for that . . . nearly.'

Niffy was already on the platform, waving at them and shouting, 'Hi! Over here!'

Once she'd hugged them all hello, she took both Min's and Gina's bags and began to head out to the car park.

The filthiest SUV Gina had ever set eyes on – was it actually white under all that mud? – was waiting for them in the car park. Mr Nairn-Bassett, in a flat tweed cap and green anorak, was perched behind the steering wheel.

'Hello, girls!' he barked out at them as Niffy opened the door. 'There's plenty of room in the back – just push the dogs out of the way.'

As soon as she heard this instruction, Min shrank back.

Niffy stuck her head in the door and yelled, 'Doughal! Macduff! Back!' And with a clatter and scamper of legs and paws, the two huge black hounds jumped over into the boot space, leaving a hairy, smelly blanket spread across the back seat for the girls to sit on.

Gina slid a pointy-booted toe carefully into the car and lowered her designer-jean-clad derrière onto the seat.

'Told you we should have dressed down,' Amy whispered to her.

But even if Gina had been warned she'd be travelling in a car like this, there was nothing in her wardrobe that would have been suitable. Even gardening at the boarding house was a problem, because Gina didn't have 'old clothes'; she just didn't do scruffy. Unlike Niffy, who was scrambling into the front passenger seat in her usual outfit of dirty black jodhpurs, a black woollen jumper that seemed to be unravelling at the sleeves and her trusty leather riding boots, caked in mud.

It was a thirty-minute journey along wet and twisty roads before the rickety Range Rover was finally bumping its way up the potholed drive to Blacklough Hall.

Gina looked out of the car window, but in the dark she could only make out the size of the place; none of the detail was visible. However, as they approached it, she saw that there was a proper grand entrance to the front door, with stone steps and balustrades. However, Mr N-B drove them straight past and round to the car park at the back of the house. The car came to a halt and the dogs and then their bags were unloaded. A small back door opened and Mrs N-B appeared.

'Girls! Good trip? Lovely to see you!' she trilled. 'So very nice of you to come and visit!'

Gina found herself being ushered into a warm and cheerful kitchen which smelled of boiling potatoes and damp dog. Like both Amy and Min, she caught herself peering a little too closely at Mrs N-B to try and gauge whether she looked any better or any worse than when they'd last seen her in the summer.

Mrs N-B looked thin, but then she always looked thin. Her tweedy skirt and pink cardigan skimmed a very slight frame. There was a pink and white scarf tied over her head, and with a wave of shock Gina registered that this was how she was disguising her lack of hair.

Niffy had warned them in an email that her mother was getting 'a bit thin on top' as a result of the chemotherapy. 'She's skinny too, but don't be fooled,' Niffy had written. 'She's as tough as old boots.'

The girls were urged to 'dump' their bags upstairs, 'freshen up' and head for the dining room.

'But don't you want some help, Mrs Nairn-Bassett?' Min protested.

'No, no,' she insisted. 'Everything is under control.'

Gina had been told to expect 'stately home in distress', but still, the dining room was something of a shock. It was a dark, dark room with navy-blue walls, large ancestral portraits, an enormous wooden table, highly polished with – at a glance – about eighteen dining chairs around it.

This was all the sort of thing that Gina had expected, but the first surprise was the cold. Opening the door to the dining room reminded her of opening the door to her fridge back home: it brought a blast of icy air. Two electric heaters had been plugged in on either side of the room, but they didn't appear to have been switched on yet; maybe that would only happen when they were sitting down.

Six places had already been set, huddled together at one end of the table, and a there was a soup tureen on the sideboard. Well, Gina guessed it was a tureen, but she couldn't be sure as it was wrapped in a piece of stripy blanket, probably to keep it warm.

Once they'd taken their seats and been served, Gina got her next surprise. The soup was disgusting! There was no other word for it. She had loaded up her spoon for the first mouthful and had to concentrate hard not to gag it back out again.

'Mmm, oxtail,' Mr N-B had murmured approvingly. 'Is that legal again now? I thought we weren't allowed to eat spine with all that CJD nonsense.'

If Gina had wanted to gag before, now she wanted to hurl.

With a clatter, Min suddenly dropped her spoon. There was a look of terror on her face, which Niffy immediately understood.

'Doughal!' she called out, sticking her head under the table to investigate. 'Come here. Leave Min alone.'

Gina now realized that this meant it was Macduff's great hairy head that she had on her lap. But she didn't want him to move; she suspected that dogs this size were rarely vicious, and anyway, with his breath on her leg and his big hot weight on her thigh, this might be the only chance she got to feel warm.

'You're not having any?' Mr N-B asked his wife sharply.

Mrs N-B had a tall glass in front of her – something greeny orange and kind of frothy.

'Now, Dad,' Niffy warned, 'you promised you weren't going to have a go.'

'I know, but' – Mr N-B crinkled his face up with displeasure – 'spinach and carrot juice?' he asked.

Mrs N-B nodded.

'Don't you think you need some protein? Something to build you up?'

'Dad . . .' Niffy said gently.

Protein and something to build it up were definitely things the chicken which was served as the next course had needed before it met its end. Amy looked at the thin, stringy strands of meat, the three green beans and two small boiled potatoes on her plate, and wondered how on earth Niffy and her brother Finn got to be the size they were if all their meals were like this. No wonder Nif loved boarding-school food so much.

'So how's your old man, Amy?' Mr N-B asked as he forked up his tiny helping of chicken with gusto. 'Does he own all the fleshpots in Glasgow yet?'

This was a really odd way of putting it, but Amy was now quite used to crusty old school types finding her dad's line of business – not to mention way of *life* – quite shockingly strange. Her dad's boyfriend . . . She wondered how she could work him into the conversation – she'd quite like to see how Mr N-B coped with that one. She wondered if he would turn as purple as the beetroot and seaweed drink that Mrs N-B was now sipping as her second course.

Gina and Min had already scraped their plates clean and Min was wondering if it would be rude to ask for a piece of bread. It had been hours and hours and hours since lunch, and she knew that what she'd eaten so far wouldn't keep her going through the night.

Both Min and Gina came from bright, hot, blue-skied countries; their homes were shiny white and clean, and lit all day long with sunshine. Both were secretly thinking how truly awful it must be to live in a place like this. Dark navy blues and browns; grim paintings hanging from the wall; and the cold, the damp, bone-chilling cold. No wonder the N-B parents were so miserable. At least Niffy had been able to come to school and escape from it all.

All the hopes that had been raised by the word 'pudding' were dashed as soon as Niffy walked in with the dish: a silver platter piled high with blackberries picked from the garden. There were green ones, light purple ones, then the odd bit of leaf and twig that suggested they hadn't even been washed.

When Gina bit into one, she pulled a face because it was so small, so gritty and so sour. She decided that, rude or not, she was going to have to leave the rest on her plate, swimming in the thin coating of single cream from the elaborate silver cow creamer.

After dinner there was coffee and some more polite chit-chat in one of the slightly more cosy sitting rooms. It had escaped no one's notice that instead of coffee Mrs N-B had produced a twig from the pocket of her cardigan and stirred it thoughtfully around a mug of boiled water before drying it carefully on a napkin and replacing it.

'Liquorice,' was all she said when her husband looked up at her and shook his head.

Anyway, once it was all over, including the clearing away, Niffy grabbed her friends by the hands and led them up several flights of stairs to the low-ceilinged former servants' wing where they were to sleep.

'Don't worry – I've got radiators, hot-water bottles

and even' – her eyes twinkled with mischief – 'an electric blanket.'

'Oh shag, I thought you were going to say a large packet of duty-free fags,' Amy sighed. 'I think that's the least we can expect after a dinner like that. I'm sorry, but you people are mad. Haven't you heard of chips? Or M&S? Or even tinned soup? I'm sorry,' she repeated, 'but where did your mum learn to cook, Nif?'

'St Jude's,' Niffy, Gina and Min answered together.

'Well, she must have been bottom of the class.' Amy sat down heavily on the saggy double bed in the middle of a room plastered in horse photos, posters, silver trophies and rosettes.

'We're in your room, I take it?' Amy asked Niffy.

'Yup. Make yourselves at home. I even have a telly.' She pointed to an ancient old set perched on top of a chest of drawers.

'No chance of cable all the way out here, though, is there?' Amy asked.

Niffy shook her head.

'Sky?' Amy asked, but she knew it was a long shot. 'A DVD player?'

When Niffy shook her head at both these suggestions, Amy couldn't help asking, 'What do you people do for fun round here?'

'We make our own, of course,' Niffy said, and with that she sprang up and went over to the chest of drawers. From the bottom drawer she carefully drew out a mammoth bar of chocolate, four paper cups, a corkscrew and a bottle of wine so dark it almost looked black.

As she set it down on the bedside table, Gina couldn't help noticing the layer of dust and the faded, brown, curling label. 'Jeez, that looks old,' she told Niffy.

'Yeah.' Niffy took a closer look at the label. 'Nineteen sixty-nine. Oops! It's from the cellar. I usually stay clear of any labels I recognize, but I thought you deserved something a little special.'

She turned the label towards Amy, who could be counted on to recognize the finer things in life. '*Château la Tour* . . .' Amy read out hesitantly. 'Yeah . . . I think that's quite good.'

'Excellent!' Niffy exclaimed, and began to set to enthusiastically with the corkscrew.

'Niffy, are you drinking a lot of wine . . . up here, on your own?' wondered Min, who came from a family of caring doctors.

'No' – Niffy shook her head – 'you don't need to worry about me, honestly. I share a sneaked bottle with Finn whenever he's home, but no, I'm not sitting up here with my hot-water bottle drinking the cellar dry.'

Min smiled. 'Glad to hear it.'

Once all the paper cups were filled, the girls found seats on the bed or the battered sofa beside it, then raised their cups in a toast.

'Cheers!'

'Now,' Amy said, as soon as the first mouthfuls had gone down, 'let's talk about boys.'

Chapter Fourteen

The paper cupfuls of wine, the cosy warmth – now that the heaters were turned up full blast – and the comforting chaos of the room itself all helped the girls to relax.

All four of them were together again; it was just like old times, familiar times. Suddenly it was easy to really talk and confide, especially for Niffy, who'd had no one to talk to properly for weeks now. Her older brother had not, like her, moved back home. He had exams to sit, so their parents wouldn't hear of him leaving his expensive boarding school, Craigiefield. They had only let Niffy come back because she had so stubbornly insisted.

'What's your new school like?' asked Gina, who had experience of moving from one place to another.

Niffy's reaction was to toss back the last of the wine in her cup before saying levelly, 'It's shit. But can we please not talk about that? Let's talk about Angus.'

'*Angus?*' Amy chimed in, making a mental note to ask Niffy all about her new school privately. 'What's happening with Angus?'

'Angus?' Min sounded mystified. She'd obviously forgotten all about the cheerful, jokey St Lennox boy who'd asked Niffy for a date at the end of the summer term.

'Oh yes, Angus!' Gina exclaimed. She remembered Angus well. 'Have you seen him?'

To their surprise, Niffy looked quite shy as she told them, 'He's got an aunt and uncle who live not far from here, and . . . well, let's just say he's been spending quite a bit of time visiting them recently.'

'Woo-hoo,' Amy teased. 'Is he providing a shoulder to lean on?'

'You could say that . . .' Niffy admitted. 'But he's not exactly handsome, is he?' she asked with a grin. 'I mean, he has a kind face but it's a bit . . . meaty.'

This caused the three others to crack up with laughter.

'But he's a really nice guy . . . and his *bod*!' she added, before anyone thought Angus was just a friend. Because he was definitely more than a friend.

'His *bod*?' Amy prompted, wanting to make sure Niffy elaborated.

'He's very sporty – lots of muscles . . .'

'And how do you know this?'

'We went swimming in the river in the summer . . . quite a lot.'

'Costumes on or off?' Amy asked incredulously.

'Mainly on,' came Niffy's reply, but her eyes were fixed shyly on the cup in her hand.

'*Mainly* on!' Amy repeated. 'Luella Nairn-Bassett!' she exclaimed, using Niffy's hated full name.

'He is *hot*,' Niffy confessed, causing surprise all round. 'You know I said last term that it was so long since I'd fancied a boy, I'd almost forgotten what it was like? Well, that's all changed.'

Gina and Amy instinctively drew a little closer to their friend. 'You realize that graphic details are required,' Amy prompted her.

'Only if you go first,' came Niffy's cheeky reply. 'Min, you might want to put your fingers in your ears.'

'No! I'm allowed to be curious,' Min told her.

'But purely in the interests of science,' Gina joked.

'Stop it!' Min exclaimed, sounding almost angry. 'Why does no one think I'll ever be interested in a boy?

Maybe you think no boy will ever be interested in *me*! Is that it?'

This caused something of a surprised silence in the room.

'We don't . . .'

'We didn't . . .'

'No, that's not . . .'

All three of her friends rushed to reassure her.

Once she had calmed down again, Niffy had to ask Amy, 'OK, you and Jason . . . How did the hot Glasgow date go?'

'We kissed . . . a lot . . .' Amy was happy to admit. 'He's totally great when he's there, right in front of me. But when we're apart, it's as if I don't exist. There's no urgency to see me again. I'm just supposed to sit about waiting for him to be in the mood for another date. And that drives me up the wall!'

'Hmmm . . . it's not balanced,' Niffy decided thoughtfully. When Amy looked at her blankly, she added, 'You like Jason more than he likes you. That's how it is. That's the truth. You either have to live with it, or move on to the next one. Maybe there's always a slight imbalance. Maybe even when people stay together happily for years and years, it's because one loves the other just slightly more and they both live with it.'

'Very philosophical,' was Min's verdict. 'So with you and Angus . . . who loves who more?'

'Aha!' Niffy went round the paper cups with a top-up of wine. 'Hard to tell at this stage. We are besotted!'

'So just how far are you two planning to go?' Amy asked, the wine making her fearlessly curious.

Niffy leaned back on her bed and thought about Angus. To say she hadn't thought about how far they might go would be a lie. His body was so heavy and so comforting to hold – his kisses and the way he made her boil up inside until she felt hot and needy for him. But . . . but . . . she was still fifteen and he was newly seventeen. Peeling off their swimsuits and pressing their bodies together had felt too extreme and had only happened once.

The next time they'd met, they had kept their suits on and hips apart. Niffy thought she'd like to really get to know Angus – maybe go out with him for a year or so – before she made a big decision like that. She wanted to trust him with herself; wanted to make sure that he really, really cared about her. But she already thought that he did. He wanted to know all about her mum, all about her school. He phoned her up twice a week every week and was incredibly kind. Yes, she had a feeling she was with her first real boyfriend.

'Mel's had sex,' Amy interrupted Niffy's thoughts. 'We had to bribe her with wine and two cigarettes but she coughed the details eventually.'

'Yeah, I bet she coughed a lot after two cigarettes,' was Min's disapproving comment.

'And . . . ?' Niffy asked. She wasn't usually curious about Mel's personal details, but now that she was thinking about this herself, she wanted to know.

'She said it was OK.' Amy gave a slight shrug of her shoulders. 'She didn't give much more info than you'd get from close reading of *Cosmo*. With sex, you obviously have to be there to really get what's going on.'

'The first time was apparently a relief because it took some time to get everything in the right place,' Gina added. 'And she couldn't get over his horrible dark-blue underwear!'

Min pulled a face and said, 'Eeuwww. I think this is all too much information.'

'But what about you, Min?' Niffy wanted to know. 'Who do you sigh about when your head hits the pillow in Iris dorm?'

To everyone's surprise, Min started to blush. She quickly tried to cover up by saying, 'No one – of course not, don't be silly!'

But when she shook her head, Amy, Niffy and Gina couldn't help feeling that there was something forced about her denial.

Maybe there *was* a boy. Someone somewhere who had sparked Min's interest for the very first time.

Chapter Fifteen

The first half of the following day didn't go so well. The girls woke up after their late-night chat to a grey sky and grey drizzle.

There was spiky smoked haddock for breakfast and blackened toast, along with weirdly burned-tasting tea.

'How did your mum manage to burn the tea?' Amy hissed under her breath at Niffy.

'It's not burned,' Niffy hissed back. 'It's Lapsang Souchong.'

'Good grief!' Amy muttered.

They'd breakfasted in the kitchen, with the Aga giving out just enough heat to keep the room above the chill in the rest of the house.

Watching Niffy ride Ginger after breakfast was about as exciting as burned toast and tea. It was obvious from the way she talked to him that she loved her horse. But standing around in a damp field in the rain watching your friend ride round and round was not exactly fun.

When Amy announced that she would buy everyone lunch in Buckthwaite, they all perked up slightly at the prospect.

But too soon. Buckthwaite turned out to be a small place with just one café, where they sat on pine benches beside steamy windows and ate soggy cheese and tomato sandwiches. It was totally depressing.

'Do you miss Edinburgh?' Gina asked Niffy.

'Yeah,' she admitted.

'Do you miss school?'

'Sort of . . . You know how it is with St Jude's,' Niffy replied. 'Can't live with it, can't live without it. You don't really want to be away from home, but then you wouldn't see any of your friends, who you love just like family' – she beamed at them all – 'so you drag yourself back there term after term.'

They'd arranged to meet the Range Rover and Mr N-B at two o'clock in the Co-op car park, when he was going to drive them over to Angus's aunt and uncle's place.

As they set off towards the car park through the unending drizzle, the girls passed a group of teenagers huddled beneath the arches of the small town hall on the high street. One of them, a girl dressed in tight jeans, a tracksuit top and a baseball cap, called out as they passed, 'Got your posh friends down for the weekend, have you, your ladyship?'

Amy, Gina and Min stopped in their tracks and looked over at the girl in astonishment. Niffy, by contrast, ducked her head down and carried on walking at a brisk pace.

'We're not good enough to talk to then, are we, your highness? Lady Toffee Nose?' a second girl, standing beside the first, chipped in with a sneer.

Amy, Gina and Min were still rooted to the spot, staring at the girls in horror.

Now the other members of the group were joining in. The boys were whistling, and there were calls of 'Stuck-up cow!' 'Snooty witch!' and 'Posh bird!'

Niffy didn't even want to wait for her friends. She just pulled her shoulders almost up to her ears and kept on walking.

Amy, Gina and Min looked at the girls, looked at each other in outrage and looked at the girls again. Gina's mouth was hanging open in shock: was this how Niffy's new classmates were treating her? No wonder she'd described school as 'shit' and didn't want to talk about it. Amy's hands were on her hips; Amy's face was clouding over with fury; Amy was very definitely about to say something loud and angry.

Gina brushed against Amy's arm. 'Maybe you shouldn't,' she warned. 'Maybe it will make things worse.'

But Amy was already taking a deep breath. 'Just what do you think you'rrrre playing at?' she fired out in her strongest Glaswegian accent. 'Our pal is at your school so she can be at home looking after her sick mum.'

No one in the group said anything for a moment, so Amy went on, not quite so angry now, 'At least give her a chance. She's a nice person. Some of you could probably be nice too . . . if we gave you a chance.'

By this time, Niffy had stopped and turned to see what was going on.

The girl who'd made the first comment spotted her and immediately shouted, 'Ooooh, you've finally turned to look at us then, Princess Poncey Pants.'

'I said *be nice*,' Amy said, slowly and icily.

'Or *what*?' The girl turned and curled her lip at her. 'What ya gonna do? Get the Queen down to have us arrested?'

This caused an outbreak of loud, sneering laughter from her friends.

Amy had been in enough playground scraps to know that it was time to retreat with a parting shot; she could come back to fight another day.

'You're going to be very sorry,' she said loudly and clearly so that everyone could catch each word. Then she took Gina and Min by the arm and marched them away from the group as quickly as she could.

The laughter and whistles of the teenagers were still ringing in their ears as they rounded the corner into the Co-op car park.

'Nice new friends,' Amy hissed at Niffy.

'Don't interfere. It's best to just keep your head down and stay out of their way.'

'No it isn't!' Amy retorted. 'You've got to sort them out or this will go on and on all the time you're at their school. And that could be a while! I promise you, you've got to sort it out.'

'No I don't,' Niffy snapped.

Mr N-B's filthy old Range Rover was already in the car park. Without saying anything more, Niffy opened the front passenger door, climbed in and slammed it shut.

Chapter Sixteen

The drive from Buckthwaite to Angus's aunt and uncle's home through green and twisty country lanes seemed to soothe Niffy. As the car turned into a long tree-lined driveway, she turned and smiled at her friends in the back seat.

'Wait till you see this place – I think you're going to be impressed,' she told them.

The driveway seemed to go on for miles, winding through leafy woodland, then past green fields where sheep grazed and enormous oak trees, protected by little wooden fences, spread their graceful branches. At the end of the drive, the rhododendron bushes fell away and they pulled up in front of a vast grey stone building.

There was no way this could be a *house*, Gina couldn't help thinking. It looked more like a museum or a school – even some kind of castle. Surely this couldn't be where Angus's relatives lived! Only royalty could afford a place like this.

In contrast to Blacklough Hall, the front doors were thrown wide open at the sound of the car on the drive. A flight of steps dotted with colourful pots of plants and flowers led up to the ornate marble-columned entrance hall.

Already there were people standing there, a middle-aged couple and, towering above them, waving frantically, a hunky blond figure, which must surely be Angus.

'Hi! Hello there! Good to see you – great to see you!' He came bounding down the steps towards them, booming out greetings, scattering three tiny yapping dogs as he went.

'Does everyone live in a place like this around here?' Gina asked Amy, only half-joking.

'Erm, no. Don't think Niffy's school pals do, for a start,' came Amy's reply.

'But look at it,' Min said, staring through the Range Rover windows in something close to dismay. 'It just doesn't feel right that someone should have a house this big. What about the homeless people?'

'You'd fit plenty of them in here,' Amy joked. As she stepped out of the car, she watched happily as Angus kissed Niffy on both cheeks – which could just have been politeness, though the hands around her waist pulling her towards him definitely weren't. And while her father wasn't looking, Angus leaned down and gave Niffy's ear a quick lick, which caused Amy to utter a shriek of surprise.

'Hey, Amy,' Angus said when he could bear to take his eyes off Niffy. 'Can I kiss you too?'

'Yeah.' Amy offered each cheek in turn, but warned him, 'Just no licking, OK?'

He ushered them in. 'Come on, meet the *rellies*.'

The rellies, Angus's aunt and uncle, turned out to be nice. The house was glittering and the unmistakable impression was: rich, rich, rich. It couldn't have been more different to the threadbare state of Blacklough.

'My uncle is a banker, you know – wads of money,' Angus explained in a cheerful whisper.

When Amy was shown into the drawing room, she made straight for the beautiful bay window and admired the three gleaming cars parked outside. An Aston for him, a Lotus for her, and an immaculate old-fashioned blue Land Rover, perfectly restored, shining and loved in every way – for going into the fields, perhaps?

'Angus, who cleans the cars here?' Amy asked.

'This old boy, Roger, he does all the odd jobs . . . Why?' he wondered.

'He does a blinking good job,' she said. Even her dad's driver, who kept the McCorquodale Jag sparkling, would be impressed. 'I need to have a little word with Rog, if that's OK,' she went on.

Angus's eyebrows shot up. 'Fine . . . but . . .'

'Niffy said you'd just passed your driving test,' she added.

'Yes,' Angus confirmed, 'but—'

'Good!' Amy told him with a secretive smile. 'Because I've just had this totally, *totally* brilliant idea.'

Chapter Seventeen

It was nearly eight p.m. and already growing dark in the village of Buckthwaite. This was exactly what Amy had wanted. Any earlier and there might have been too much daylight to get away with her plan; any later and there was a danger that the people they needed to see would have gone home.

'There!' Amy pointed, feeling a rush of nerves. 'There they are . . . That's definitely *her* anyway, the ring-leading cow. So long as we make an impression with her, this will work. OK, pump up the bass.'

Molly Haddon – that was the name of the mouthy girl in the baseball cap who'd had a go at Niffy earlier that day – was one of the first of the group to spot the white Range Rover coming up the street towards the arches of the town hall, where they were still huddled.

How could she not notice it? Amy, Niffy, Gina, Min and Angus had spent *hours* cleaning it. Mr N-B had agreed, of course, but even he'd been astonished by the degree of effort which they had all put into the task.

Amy had charmed Roger into handing over car shampoo, T-Cut colour restorer (which the Nairn-Bassett Range Rover had needed, that was for sure), wax polish, chrome buffer, tyre blackener, glass polisher, even a hand-held vacuum for the seats.

'Come on!' Amy had urged them over and over during the cleaning process. 'It's got to shine! I know how these things are done. It can't look like it's ever spent one second outside the inner city.'

Once the Range Rover had been polished to perfection, Amy had enlisted Angus's help to gather together all the other items she needed.

'The car's CD player works, doesn't it?'

'Hmm . . .' Niffy didn't know. 'Dad always listens to Radio Three.'

When inspection of the CD player had revealed that it did in fact function, Angus had been sent to rifle through his cousin's old CD collection until they'd found exactly the right thing.

'*Shake Da House* vol. six – perfect!' Amy had declared as she set the CD aside.

Then thin chiffon scarves were tied over three big

torches so they gave off glowing purple, blue and yellow lights.

'And now for our disguises,' Amy had announced, causing the four faces of the others to turn to her in disbelief. She still hadn't told them what she had in mind. She was worried that if she told them, they would refuse to play along and simply think that she was out of her mind. But somewhere, deep down, she just absolutely knew they could pull this off.

'OK, now we need baseball caps, puffy anoraks, sunglasses, and lots and lots of gold chains,' Amy had told them.

'*What?*' Angus had demanded in astonishment. 'Where the hell are we going to get all that? And why? Why don't you just tell us what's going on?'

'Look at the size of this place!' Amy had insisted, refusing to be put off. 'If we start looking round here, I promise you we'll find everything we need. We'll raid the fancy-dress boxes, the backs of wardrobes – even the Christmas decorations if we have to! Come on!'

'Look at that.' Molly Haddon was now nudging the girl next to her, and most of the others turned to look in the direction of her pointed finger. 'That's pretty flash.'

Now all eyes were fixed on the white Range Rover as it drew closer. All four of the 4X4's side windows were half-open so that the teens standing on the wet pavement could hear the loud music *thump, thump, thump*ing from inside.

'That *is* flash,' one of the boys agreed with Molly.

They were looking at the cool coloured lights that seemed to glow from the car windows, lighting it from within.

'It's a customized one,' the boy added. 'Special light and sound system,' he muttered with a hint of longing. 'That is *unbelievably* cool.'

Now the car was drawing closer, slowing right down; to their surprise, it was pulling to a halt right beside them.

In the passenger's seat they could see an incredibly glamorous blonde, heavily made up, wearing dark glasses, flashing with diamonds, her hair falling loose about her shoulders. In the driver's seat was a massive guy in a big padded anorak, baseball cap and large dark glasses. He looked very blond and very serious. In the back seat was another seriously padded guy, also in a baseball cap and shades. In his hand was some sort of thick wooden stick – like a bat or something.

'Maybe they're Russians,' the boy wondered out

loud. He sounded almost nervous. But then this was Buckthwaite: exotic strangers in customized Range Rovers weren't exactly common around here.

When the passenger window slid down, the group of teenagers instinctively took a step back.

The blonde girl in the front seat turned to face them. She raised her sunglasses so that she could take a better look at them all.

'Remember me, then, guys?' she asked in clear, unmistakably Glaswegian tones.

It took a moment or two, but then Molly and her friends realized that this was the same girl who'd been in the high street earlier with that stuck-up Luella Nairn-Bassett girl. Every one of them was now too nervous to make any sort of reply to Amy.

'Do you know who my dad is?' she began. 'No, I don't think you do. Well, let me tell you. My dad is one of the hardest men in Glasgow. No!' she scolded. 'Don't look in the car. He's not in the car. You think he'd drive around in a tin can like this? No, he drives a really nice set of wheels,' she went on, not even remotely nervous now.

When she was ordinary Amy McCorquodale, she wasn't a very good liar, but when she was in costume, playing a part, it was a different story. She was an actress now, speaking her lines with conviction, just like she'd practised all the way here.

'He's a businessman,' she said darkly. 'I don't think I need to tell you what kind of business. Let's just say he has a lot of security men . . . ready to provide *security*' – she paused and looked at them meaning-fully – 'at a moment's notice.'

Then Amy carefully opened the tiny, but oh-so-obviously-labelly handbag on her lap and took out her dinky little phone. 'I could just give him a wee call and my two security men here might have some new orders.'

Molly was now looking at her with undisguised terror, her mouth open. 'I'm . . . I'm . . . I didn't . . .' she stammered, unable to get the words out.

'It's very simple . . .' Amy had to admit she was almost enjoying this now. 'Just be nice,' she instructed, 'or at the very least *polite* to my friend Luella. Or else I might have to get some of *my* friends to give some of *your* friends a lesson in manners. And you wouldn't like that. Do you understand?'

There was an outbreak of unanimous nodding amongst the group on the pavement.

At that, Amy pressed the button on the Range Rover's electric window and felt a rush of relief when the glass slid up. Angus put the engine in gear and drove off as smoothly as he could, his palms sweating at the thought of accidentally stalling the car at this critical stage.

The three had barely made it round the corner before they collapsed into hysterics with relief. Both Niffy, heavily disguised, in the back seat and Angus in the front pulled off their baseball caps and whooped with laughter.

'You were brilliant,' Niffy told Amy. 'For goodness' sake!' she instructed. 'Go left, Angus! Left just here, otherwise we'll be back on the high street and they'll see us!'

Chapter Eighteen

On Monday evening, just as Min was reaching over to switch off her bedside light and plunge Iris dorm into darkness, she voiced the question that everyone else had been thinking about all evening:

'Do you think Niffy got on OK at school today?'

'Dunno,' Gina and Amy replied together.

'No one else has heard from her then?'

'No,' they answered together again.

'Well . . . we'll just have to wait and see,' Min said, and then, with a click, it was dark.

Gina closed her eyes, but after a few minutes she opened them again and listened to the sounds around her.

Amy was rustling about in her bed, pulling the duvet tightly around her and snuggling down into her favourite sleeping position. Min was quiet as a mouse, as usual, but outside in the brightly lit corridor Gina could hear the older girls, who didn't have to be in bed yet, coming and going, making the stiff hinges of the fire doors creak.

Like most of the other boarders, Gina had got used to the sounds of the boarding house and could usually fall asleep quickly, tuning them out. But tonight her mind seemed to be restlessly turning from one subject to the next and she had the feeling that it wasn't going to be so easy to sleep.

She thought about her little brother. In a few days' time it would be Menzie's birthday, and although she'd bought him a present, wrapped and parcelled it up and sent it to the States in plenty of time, she wasn't going to be there. This was the first birthday of her brother's that she had ever missed. That made her think of the day he'd come home from the hospital, in her stepdad's arms so that her mother could swoop down, scoop Gina up and soothe her prickling jealousy with the words: 'Congratulations, Gina! You're a sister. You're a beautiful big sister and your baby brother is going to love you.'

It didn't matter that her mum and her three Californian school friends would be coming over to Scotland to see her soon; Gina could suddenly feel tears forming behind her eyes, but she quickly squeezed them away, not wanting anyone to hear her cry. And that was when Dermot came into her mind, without her even asking him to . . . or so it seemed.

They hadn't even fallen out over Scarlett, whoever she was. They'd fallen out over Charlie the idiot Fotheringham and his stupid, stupid, nasty little remarks. Well, fine. Dermot was probably with Scarlett now, and it was just as well that Gina had untangled herself from him as quickly as possible. Two fat tears fell silently from the corners of her eyes, slid down the sides of her face and landed on the scratchy white cotton of the boarding-house pillowcase.

When she finally fell asleep, Gina tossed and turned, troubled by vivid dreams of a techno-coloured California, then found herself wide awake in the silent darkness.

The winking red numbers of her alarm clock showed that it was 1.56 a.m. Despite the dark, Gina could just make out Min quietly getting up and heading out of the room, pulling the door shut noiselessly behind her. Five minutes later and Min still hadn't come back in. After fifteen minutes Gina was beginning to worry. Was Min sleepwalking? She put on her dressing gown and slippers and decided to go and investigate.

First of all Gina checked the bathroom, but there was no one in there. Then it occurred to her that there was only one place in the boarding house where Min was truly comfortable and at home; one place where she liked to spend the majority of her waking hours: the study. If Min was sleepwalking, then she would definitely sleepwalk all the way down there.

As quietly as she could, Gina hurried down the stairs and along the silent corridors. As she approached the large double doors, she saw a sliver of light underneath them, but still, she made her way in quietly.

A single small lamp had been switched on over one of the computer desks; the only sound was the quiet tippity-tap of fast typing. Gina could see her friend's dark head bent over one of the computer keyboards. But Min was so busy typing, she hadn't even heard her come into the room.

So Gina began to walk towards her desk. She didn't mean to give Min a fright, but Min was so engrossed in what she was doing that she didn't notice Gina until she was hovering right behind her.

'Hi,' Gina said quietly.

'Aaargh!' Min gave a small shriek in response.

'So is this the secret of your amazing new biology grades?'

'Oh no!' was Min's response. 'You saw!' She scrambled with her mouse to close down the file she had been working on.

Gina had only meant that she'd caught Min studying in the middle of the night, but now that Min was acting all guilty and as if she'd seen something secret, out of burning curiosity she had to play along.

'So how long's this been going on?' she asked without the slightest idea what she was talking about.

'A few weeks . . .' Min confessed, blushing furiously. 'Well, about five weeks. We've not met yet, but his emails are lovely and they've really helped me so much.'

Gina was so surprised by this revelation she could hardly form her next question. *His emails are lovely . . .* What was Min talking about?

'Who is he?' she asked, astonished.

'He's this nice guy – I think he's a student. He knows loads and loads about biology and, more importantly, he's into NLP and he's giving me info on techniques to overcome my squeamishness.'

'What's NLP?' Gina was crouching down beside her

friend now, amazed to see her looking so alert and excited at two in the morning.

'Neuro-linguistic programming,' came the answer.

'OK, never mind that. Tell me about the guy?' Gina asked.

'Well, he calls himself Gecko and I call myself Raven – we've not even done real names yet.'

'Min, this is scaring me,' Gina confessed. 'Internet chat rooms, cyber dates . . . I take it you know how many weirdos are out there?'

'Don't be silly! We're just email-pals, the way people used to have pen-pals. But he seems so nice. I'd really like to meet him in person.'

'Min' – Gina sounded very serious – 'if you arrange to meet this guy, you have to do it in a very public place and at least one of us has to come with you. It's the Internet, Min!' she warned her. 'There are a lot of strange people online.'

'Gina!' Min laughed. 'He's a science geek. We got chatting through an online science club.'

'Min, promise me . . .' Gina warned.

'I'll promise you if you'll promise me not to tell Amy anything about this,' Min countered.

'Why not? She'll be happy for you.'

'No! She'll tease me – she'll go on about my geeky

Gecko boyfriend, and it's not like that!' Min insisted. 'We're just science buddies, chatting about exam problems and my anxieties about dissected frogs.'

'Well, OK,' Gina agreed, only because she knew Min was totally right. If Amy knew anything about this, she'd be like a dog with a bone.

'Why do you have to email him in the middle of the night though?' she wondered.

'It's the only time I can be sure of getting online at the same time as him,' Min answered.

'But what about sleep?'

'Oh . . . we only do this two or three times a week.'

'Two or three times a week?' Gina was astonished. 'Min, you must be exhausted!'

Min looked up at her with a confidential smile. 'I find that the back row of Miss Ballantyne's history class is the ideal place for a catch-up snooze.'

'Come on,' Gina instructed. 'Call the science club meeting to an end and let's get to bed.'

It didn't escape her notice that Min's email ended with a lot of 'x's. This was all a very interesting development and Gina had no idea how she was going to keep it a secret.

Chapter Nineteen

Mrs MacDuff, the biology teacher, was walking towards Min's seat with a curious look on her face.

'Asimina,' she began, placing Min's homework sheets down on the table, 'this is excellent work. *Unbelievably* good.'

There was slightly too much stress on the *unbelievably* for Gina's liking.

'I'm working really hard, Mrs MacDuff,' Min replied. 'I'm really trying to make progress.'

'So no one else is helping you?' the teacher wanted to know. 'There's no one else's hand in this homework?'

'No, not at all.' Min looked up and met Mrs MacDuff's gaze.

'Hmmm . . .' was all the teacher said before returning to her desk.

Was Gina imagining it or did she see some hint of

a confused blush creeping over Min's cheeks? Her eyes were cast down now and she was fiddling with her hair.

All last year, biology had been a problem for Min. But as the teacher had noticed, something had definitely changed. Gina now knew about the Internet friend who was helping Min out and she actually wished she didn't. Was geeky Gecko helping Min with her feelings about biology? Or helping her with her actual homework? Was Min cheating? And was any of this even Gina's business?

Gina wondered if she should speak to Amy – if Amy wasn't too busy hanging out with Rosie, of course; but then Gina caught sight of the classroom clock and felt a fresh pang of gloom.

Menzie would be waking up on the morning of his ninth birthday right now and she didn't even know what he had planned for the rest of the day. Would he be splashing about in the pool with a gaggle of friends? At some point he would definitely be blowing out candles on one of the fabulous chocolate cakes her mom always had specially made by the neighbourhood French pâtisserie.

When she was at school, Gina tried not to think of her family going about their daily lives without her.

It was too sad to imagine them carrying on, not knowing her new friends or the day-to-day details of her new life.

They'd never seen her dorm, except in the photos she'd emailed home; they'd never met Mrs Knebworth – or Amy, Niffy and Min, or . . . Dermot. There he was again, popping unbidden into her head, quickly she tried to press some sort of mental delete button to get rid of him.

She'd decided to phone Menzie just as soon as she could get to the boarding-house payphone. She wanted to speak to him and wish him happy birthday as early as she could. At 4 p.m. it would be 8 a.m. in LA; if she hurried, she could still catch him before he went to school.

As soon as her last lesson had finished, Gina rushed back to the boarding house, dumped her things and dialled her long internationally coded home number.

It rang and rang and rang out. Finally she hung up and tried her mother's mobile, knowing they'd only be able to speak for a moment or two because the credit on her phone card would be used up so quickly.

'Lorelei Winkelmann,' her mother answered in her most businesslike tone.

'Hi, Mom, it's me! I just wanted to wish Menzie happy birthday.'

'Oh, baby, hi!' came the faint voice way down the other end of the line. 'I'm sorry, I've just dropped him off at breakfast club. I have a really early meeting today. I'll tell him you called. He'll be out of school at four, so try him at home then. Baby, I have to go,' her mother added. 'Is everything OK?'

'Yeah . . . love you,' Gina answered quickly, because there just wasn't time to talk about how nothing felt OK now. She'd have to wait for eight whole hours before she could speak to her brother. It felt terrible! She'd have to ask Mrs Knebworth for special permission to stay up late enough. But what would her mom understand about any of this anyway? Busy, busy Mom and her early meeting.

'Love you too,' her mother answered cheerfully.

Click. Then the line was dead.

Gina replaced the receiver, feeling a hard lump of sadness in her throat. She was homesick. That's how homesickness came – in unexpected tidal waves that washed over you and made you wish and wish that like Dorothy in *The Wizard of Oz* you could click your heels three times and find yourself in your own back yard, surrounded by the people who loved you best.

It was hard to be so far away from them. But the feeling would pass, Gina knew this. It was like a dizzy spell: you had to close your eyes and breathe deeply for a few minutes and it would pass. So she was startled when the phone began to ring loudly, the sound rattling around the little telephone cubicle.

She picked up the receiver and gave a husky 'Hello?'

'Hello, could I speak to Gina Peterson please?'

There was no mistaking the warm male voice. It was Dermot.

Gina was caught off guard and wasn't sure what to say next. She was so stunned, she didn't even know if she could say *anything*. For a moment she thought she'd pretend to be someone else and get out of the phone call.

'Gina?' she began shakily, trying to disguise her voice and intending to say, *Could you call back later?*

'Gina?' Dermot repeated. 'It's you, isn't it?'

'Erm . . . yes,' she answered awkwardly.

'Were you trying to pretend it wasn't? I don't blame you,' he went on, before she had to make any stupid excuses for herself. 'I'm not exactly a catch, am I? Boring boy who works in café and rudely storms off when you want to be nice to him.'

He gave something of a gulp at the end of this and

171

Gina suspected he was just as nervous as she was.

'I do occasionally make jokes though,' he added. 'That's my redeeming feature. Jokes – though they are usually bad ones.'

'They're not,' Gina was quick to protest. 'I quite like your jokes.'

'*Quite?* You *quite* like them?' Dermot asked. 'I think I'd better hang up now – there's no way you're going to come out with me, is there?'

But Gina could hear the warmth in his voice ... and she was unwinding, relaxing, basking in that warmth as if it was a ray of sunshine beaming out of the receiver at her.

He was going to ask her out again! If she was really, *really* lucky. They were going to have another chance at being together.

'I might,' she told him, teasing a little herself now, 'if you asked me on the right kind of date.'

'Oh no! No! Don't say that. The pressure!' Dermot joked. 'I can't take the pressure. I'm sweating here.'

'Well,' Gina broke in, thinking that maybe she could make this easier for him, 'you know that exhibition at the Modern Art Gallery ... and the cakes?'

'Oh yes – no forgetting the cakes.'

'Well, maybe we could do that? On Sunday? And I'll

try and come in and see you on Saturday afternoon . . . if that's OK?'

Suddenly she remembered him telling her coldly to just forget it. 'You're sure you want to do this?' she asked him quickly, because she didn't think she could cope with being told no by him again.

'Yeah, I'm sure,' he said. 'I'm really sorry about that last time. I was just wound up. I didn't mean it.'

'Sure.' Gina let him off. 'So Saturday at the café . . . if I can make it, and Sunday, say two-thirty? At the gallery?'

'Yeah! Excellent!'

Yeah! Excellent! was just what Gina was thinking as she hurried up to Iris dorm after the phone call, a big smile plastered across her face, to tell Amy about this latest exciting development in the Gina/Dermot saga. Scarlett? Scarlett was nothing now. Well, no, that wasn't true: *Scarlett* was already a pile of notes, dialogue and scenes coming together in a little notebook on her desk in the boarding-house study room.

When she burst into the dorm, she found Min lying on her bed, nose buried in some textbook, and Amy at her chest of drawers, about to tackle one of her favourite chores: the tidying and rearranging of her lovely luxury items. She even had a little face-cloth in her hand, so she could polish her make-up cases and the expensive gold-topped bottles of cleanser and moisturizer.

'What's up?' Amy asked, her eyes on the blue and gold leather box that held her prized diamond pendant. It had been quite a few days since she'd worn it last – in fact Amy suddenly couldn't remember exactly when she'd last felt the cool touch of the gold palm tree against her neck. Just to reassure herself, and to cast a satisfied smile on those lovely stones, she took the box in her hand and gently eased open the lid.

'I've got a date with Dermot,' Gina began excitedly. 'He phoned! We've made up and he wants to go out on—'

But she couldn't finish her sentence because Amy's sharp gasp cut right across it.

'*Aargh!*'

Both Min and Gina looked over with concern. Had Amy hurt herself?

She was staring at the box in disbelief. 'It's empty!' she exclaimed, horrified. 'My necklace has gone!'

'No!' Min was the first to speak. 'It *can't* have!'

'Maybe you put it somewhere else?' Gina suggested; then, realizing how shocked her friend was, she offered, 'I'll help you look. Where else could it be?'

The next twenty minutes were spent in a panicky but nevertheless thorough search of Amy's jewellery boxes, Amy's drawers, the dorm wardrobe, even the pockets of all Amy's clothes.

Finally they had to admit that the necklace wasn't there.

Amy was on the verge of tears. 'I *loved* it!' she exclaimed. 'I just loved it so much. It was the first piece of really special jewellery that my dad has ever bought for me! Oh, God! Where has it gone? Where could it be?'

After another frantic search of every possible location and hiding place in the dorm, Amy flung herself down on her bed and, in a burst of sadness and fury, cried out, 'Why do I get the feeling that Penny Boswell-Hackett has something to do with this?'

Chapter Twenty

Lockers at St Jude's weren't locked, but they were still private. It just didn't do to go looking in other people's lockers. It wasn't a school rule, but it was part of the school code. If anyone ever looked in someone else's locker, they needed the owner's permission and a very good reason – or else serious trouble would follow.

So the next day, when classes ended, Amy and Gina felt ill at ease hanging about in the Upper Fifth locker room.

'What are we going to say we're here for?' Gina asked nervously. 'You know . . . if someone sees us.'

'*If* someone sees us,' Amy repeated with emphasis, 'then we say we're waiting for someone who's at music practice because we're walking into town with them. Honestly, this will take two minutes. Don't be such a baby!'

'I'm not!' Gina snapped, then added, 'If I'm such a

baby, maybe you should have got your little mini-me, Rosie, to come and do this job with you.'

'Oh shut up, Gina,' said Amy. 'Rosie's driving me up the wall.' Almost under her breath, she muttered, 'How do you let someone know you don't want to see quite so much of them without being really mean?'

'I don't know,' Gina told her snippily. 'I guess it's not a problem I've had: being sooooo popular.'

'Shut up,' Amy snapped again. 'Just stand at the door and make sure the coast is clear. That's all I'm asking you to do. You aren't going to have your hands in the till; you aren't going to be in trouble if someone comes in . . . *If,*' Amy repeated when she saw the worried look on Gina's face.

She had already searched through Penny's desk in the lunch break and now she was going to search her locker.

She didn't hold out much hope. The thing about day girls was that they went home. If they had stolen your prized possessions, they weren't going to leave them hanging around the school for long, were they? No. They were going to run home with them as fast as their little legs could carry them.

Still, Amy had reasoned, she had to do *something*. She had ransacked the entire Iris dorm to no avail. She had put up MISSING! posters all over the boarding house. The necklace was definitely stolen.

'Yes, *stolen*,' she kept telling her friends. 'Diamond necklaces do not get *lost*.'

Penny had it. She was convinced of that! Somehow she must have taken her necklace off or dropped it, and then Penny had got hold of it. Anyone else would have given Amy her necklace back.

'OK, I can't see anyone,' Gina announced, reluctant to be drawn into this.

The door of Penny's locker was now open and Amy was surprised to see so many books and stacks of paper in front of her.

'Oh, *mince*!' she exclaimed. 'Half the contents of the school library are in here – it's going to take me ages to search through all this.'

'Well, search quickly,' Gina hissed.

Amy speedily began to empty the locker. She hated Penny so much, she almost didn't want to touch her things. She certainly did not, under any circumstances, want to be caught doing this.

'What *is* all this stuff?' she asked as she began to sort through the papers.

'Just hurry up – you're looking for a necklace, not reading *Penny: The Collected Works*,' Gina snapped.

The locker was empty now. There were books, papers, a hockey stick, a school cardigan and an umbrella on the floor beside it. Amy ran a hand over the shelves just to double check, but there was nowhere that a diamond necklace could be hidden. She hadn't really expected to find it though, had she?

She replaced the hockey stick, the umbrella and the cardigan. Then she lifted up the first of the books, intending to put them back. It was just something about the words printed on the papers between them that caught her eye:

An original work by . . .

She stopped and gave it some consideration. She fanned the papers out in her hand: *The Dinner, an original work by Tim O'Malley*, and then, on freshly printed sheets beside them, *Dinner with Peter, by Penny B-H*. Amy began to read. By page two, ignoring the hisses from Gina, she knew that Penny was rewriting some not-very-well-known play to enter into the house drama competition.

She was cheating!

'Come and look at this!' Amy instructed Gina. 'C'mon – I'll keep watch at the door. I just need to know I'm not imagining this and that Penny Boswell-Hackett really *is* cheating. Come on!' She thrust the pages into Gina's hands and took over at the door look-out post.

Gina turned them over, taking in the similarities between the two plays. Yes, many of the words had been changed but the sense still remained the same.

'*Sit down, Mr Pym, and let me pour you a glass of wine,*' for instance, had been turned into: '*Mr Baker, take a seat and let me get you a drink.*' And so it went on for the whole page.

'Ohmigod!' Gina muttered under her breath. 'I can't believe she'd do this. Does she honestly think no one will notice? That no one in the entire school has ever heard of this writer?'

Amy came over and read out the name of the real playwright: 'Tim O'Malley – well, he doesn't sound that well known. She's hoping she'll get away with it.'

At that moment Gina looked up into Penny's locker and spied the hockey stick. 'That's a hockey stick,' she said to Amy anxiously.

'Yes! You're really coming on, Gina. Soon you'll be able to recognize a lacrosse stick too,' Amy joked back.

'That's Penny's hockey stick' – Gina was pointing at the locker now – 'and didn't Niffy send us an email to say there was a Scottish team hockey practice but she wasn't going to come up to it . . . And wasn't it on Wednesday evening? Which would be today?'

Amy looked at the stick now. It was very shiny and new. There wasn't a scrape or a scratch or a single graze on the smooth wooden head. It was brand new. A very expensive model. The kind of thing a proud parent might buy their daughter as a present for making it into the Scottish hockey team.

'OK, I think we should just pack these things away now,' Amy said briskly. 'Just to be on the safe side . . . But I'm sure she's not going to come back here now.'

As they re-packed the locker hastily, they were startled by the sound of a door opening further down the corridor; and now footsteps were approaching – at a run.

'Quick!' Amy instructed, snatching the books and papers from Gina and trying to bundle them back into the locker as fast as she possibly could.

But the locker-room door had now flown open, and although Amy tried to slam Penny's locker shut, there were too many things in the way and it just bounced straight back open again.

'Just what the hell do you think you're doing?' came the enraged shout.

Both Gina and Amy were horrified to see the one

girl they did not want there, staring at them in shock.

'What are you doing?' Penny Boswell-Hackett repeated furiously. 'That's my locker! You sneaky little thieves!'

Amy immediately went over to confront Penny. 'How dare you?' she stormed back. 'Something very valuable has been stolen from me. I looked in your locker because I was sure you'd know something about it.'

Now Penny looked even more furious, her face flushed and her eyes flashing at Amy. 'Why would I want to take anything from *you*?' she stormed. 'What on earth do you think you've got that I would even want!'

'A beautiful diamond necklace,' Amy replied.

At this, a quite genuine look of surprise crossed Penny's face. 'I don't *want* your necklace. I don't *have* your necklace. I don't know *anything* about it,' she said coldly. 'And I'm going to report you for going through my locker.'

'No, you're not.' Gina spoke up for the first time.

'Keep your nose out of it!' Penny snapped at her.

'Yeah, but you're not,' Gina continued steadily, 'because we've found something of yours that proves you are still a thief.'

'What are you talking about?' Penny came towards her, frowning.

'Here . . .' Amy reached into the locker and brought out the incriminating typed pages. She thrust them in Penny's direction.

Both girls could see Penny recoil in shock.

'Wh-what? What do you mean?' she stammered, then recovered. 'That's just homework.' She snatched the pages out of Amy's hand.

'I don't think so,' Gina told her. 'I think you'll find that's plagiarism. Ever heard of it? Go look it up.'

'What are you talking about?' Penny continued to defend herself.

'I think you know exactly what I'm talking about. You're taking quite a chance, aren't you, that Mrs Parker has never ever heard of Tim O'Malley?' Gina kept her voice steady.

'What are you talking about?' Penny repeated, desperately clinging to her pretence of ignorance. She brushed past them, flung the papers into her locker and got out her hockey stick. 'I'm *late*!' she shouted.

'Fine!' Amy said, her voice also raised. 'You don't mention our locker search to anyone and we won't mention O'Malley.'

Penny turned on her heel and left the room without another word.

When the door had slammed behind her, there was silence until Amy turned to Gina and admitted, 'OK, I don't think it was her.' With an angry glare, she added, 'But then who was it? I've *got* to find out!'

Chapter Twenty-one

'Just a coffee is fine for me,' Gina insisted as she and Dermot stood at the counter in the Modern Art Gallery café. She'd had to tell the Neb she was gathering research for a project Amy and Min weren't doing so she could meet him here.

'No cake?' Dermot protested. 'You can't come here and not eat the cake! It's not humanly possible.'

Gina looked once again at the glass-fronted shelves of food in front of her. The cakes, she had to admit, looked great. No, the cakes looked fantastic. There was carrot cake weighed down with a thick layer of cream-cheese frosting. There were fat blueberry muffins bursting out of their paper cases. Most tempting of all was the dark, shiny, downright sinful chocolate cake.

Dermot had already ordered a thick slice but Gina was wearing tight, tight jeans for this date and she had to think about how she was going to get into them – not just today but in future.

'Erm, no . . .' She hesitated. 'I'll just have a mouthful of yours.'

'Oh, you will?' Dermot asked playfully.

Despite her protests, he insisted on paying for her coffee, teasing, 'It's OK, I know I don't have my own swimming pool, but I can afford a round of coffees.'

A comment that made her blush right to the roots of her hair. 'Don't,' she told him off. 'Don't go on about that stuff. It doesn't matter.'

They'd already spent nearly an hour and a half touring the white rooms together, admiring the works of art, and this was the first time Dermot had made any reference to Gina being from a family that was so much wealthier than his.

It didn't matter, Gina saw now. She had made it into a much bigger deal than it was.

When they sat down at a table for two, Dermot pushed his cake towards her and she saw that he had picked up two forks.

'Don't be shy,' he insisted, and she returned his smile.

His eyes were maybe even more sparkly blue and his smile twice as infectious as she'd remembered.

As she picked up the fork and helped herself to a

small corner of the cake, Dermot asked if she was having fun.

When she nodded, the mouthful of cake making further speech impossible, he scraped off some icing for himself, then told her very sincerely, 'You know, I'm not proposing a banking merger or anything like that – you don't need to worry about my prospects . . . or my background. I just like you, and it's really good to hang out with you. Can we just take it from there?'

Although Gina felt herself blushing deeply again, she nodded and told him, 'Yeah, that sounds cool.'

'So are we allowed to make another date?' Dermot asked tentatively. 'Or would that be rushing it?'

'No, I'd like to see you again,' she admitted. 'I'd like to see lots more of you.'

At this Dermot jokily pulled up his sweatshirt sleeve and said, 'This much more, baby?'

As they left the gallery together, Dermot took her hand, casually and naturally. Gina didn't look down or say anything about it, just held his hand back, slotted her fingers between his and realized that the light, bubbly feeling in her stomach was extreme happiness.

As they went past the glass doors of the gallery shop, Gina was stopped in her tracks by the sight of Amy looking through the racks of posters.

Except that just then the blonde head turned in her direction and Gina saw that it wasn't Amy, it was Rosie. Her hair was bundled up on her head, just like Amy's today, plus she was wearing a leather jacket, just like Amy's, red leather boots and tight jeans . . . just like Amy's.

As soon as Rosie saw Gina, she smiled and waved.

Gina smiled back and prepared to walk on, her hand still cosy and snug in Dermot's, but Rosie beckoned her over.

'There's someone I know in there who wants to say hello,' Gina explained to Dermot.

'No problem,' he replied, and followed her in, still not letting her hand drop.

'Hi, Rosie,' Gina greeted the younger girl. 'Buying something for your wall?'

'I'm so glad you're here. Now I can ask you: is this the poster that Amy has hanging above her bed? Or is it this one?'

Rosie flicked the rack open at one bright blue Matisse print and then again at a second. It didn't take Gina a moment to point out the right one, because her bed was opposite Amy's, so she had spent a lot of time looking at the painting.

'Are you buying it for someone?' she asked.

'Yeah, myself,' Rosie said. 'I want it to hang above my bed too. I think it's gorgeous. Amy's got such great style, hasn't she?'

Gina looked at Rosie carefully, taking in the hairstyle, the jacket, the jeans, the boots, even the little handbag Rosie was carrying: they were all exactly the same as her friend's.

'Yeah,' she answered, 'she does, but everyone has to do their own thing . . . I guess.'

Rosie just smiled back and didn't seem to take this as any sort of comment or criticism. 'So . . . Jason . . .' she asked next. 'Is Amy still seeing him, or is he now . . . ?' Her question tailed off.

'Available?' Gina asked accusingly.

Rosie coloured up a little at this. 'No!' she said quickly. 'That wasn't what I meant.'

'I hope not,' Gina told her. 'Jason means a lot to Amy – too much really.'

'Yeah, I suppose,' Rosie replied.

Once Gina had said goodbye to Rosie, she and Dermot walked out of the gallery. As they were strolling through the peaceful green sculpture gardens, a worrying thought came into her mind. If Rosie was trying to copy Amy in every single way, could she have taken . . . well, maybe just 'borrowed' Amy's precious necklace?

'That's a very serious face,' Dermot told her. 'You're not thinking of chucking me again, are you?'

'No!' She gave him a quick smile so he would know that he didn't need to worry about that.

'Good,' he replied, then turned and with his fore-finger drew her chin gently up so that her face was tilted towards him.

When he moved in to kiss her, everyone else in the sculpture garden seemed to melt away, and for a few precious moments it was as if Gina and Dermot were the only people in the entire world.

But finally they had to break off, and after glancing at his watch, Dermot reluctantly said that he really would have to go. He swung his rucksack off his shoulder, telling her he was going to write down the names of some of the Californian artists she'd been talking about, so he could look them up.

That was cute, she couldn't help thinking as he rummaged in his bag and brought out a scruffy little diary. He was so into her, he was going to look up things she'd been talking about!

He opened the diary and pulled a stubby little pencil from its spine. 'Now, Lloyd Wright . . .' he began. 'How do I spell that?'

Gina looked down at the page he was balancing on

his knee and began to spell. As her eye travelled to another entry written in red right across one of the dates, she saw something that made the words she'd intended to say next – *Dermot, do you want to come to our Halloween party?* – die in her mouth unspoken.

Quite clearly in his diary, Gina could read the scrawled words: *Scarlett tonight.*

Chapter Twenty-two

When Gina arrived back at the boarding house that afternoon, she rushed to find Amy.

This wasn't to talk about Scarlett. Scarlett was something so private and awful and hurtful and confusing that she didn't think she'd ever be able to mention it to anyone. How could Dermot look at her with so much affection, kiss her so amazingly, sound so desperate to see her again and yet have an evening date with Scarlett? How could that be?

And anyway, Amy would tell her to do the perfectly obvious thing, the one thing she couldn't bring herself to do . . . Amy would say: *Stop messing around, you dimwit. Ask him who the hell Scarlett is!*

But then it was so easy to give other people advice, wasn't it?

Gina would quite like to tell Amy to stop being such a dimwit herself. Jason was not worthy. No way!

Amy was in the common room, where she'd managed to snatch some time to catch up on her email on one of the school computers.

'Hi! How are your dad, Niffy and Jason?' Gina asked, guessing that this was who Amy was getting in touch with.

Amy greeted her friend with a smile. 'Had a nice little date, have we? Had a nice little smoochy-woochy in the arty gardens?'

'Yes thank you,' Gina said simply, hoping she looked as happy as she should.

'My dad is fine,' Amy replied, leaving out details of the argument she was still having with him about Jason. 'Niffy is in Edinburgh next week for a team practice, but it's on Wednesday so I doubt we'll be able to get out to see her. But her mum's doing well . . . And Jason, hah!' she groaned. 'Busy this weekend, of course, but he's going to try and come to the Halloween party and he says he'll definitely meet me during the afternoon before it . . . so, you know, another week goes by.'

'Where does he want to meet?' Gina asked.

'I said the Arts Café, so I won't look like a total spod when he's half an hour late. You'll come too, won't you?' Amy wheedled. 'To see your lover boy again.'

'Don't call him that,' Gina told her, but couldn't stop the blush from creeping up her neck. 'Anyway, I'm here because there's something I want to talk to you about.'

'Yeah?' Amy swivelled back on her desk chair, then hopped up and headed over towards the kettle. 'Tea?' she asked.

'No, thanks,' Gina answered, letting herself drop into one of the squashy sofas. 'I've had enough caffeine and adrenaline for one day.'

'So . . .' Amy busied herself with the whole mug and tea-bag thing. 'What's up?'

'Have you noticed how much Rosie is copying you these days?' Gina asked.

'Erm, well . . . not really, I don't think,' Amy said, but this was a fib. How could *anyone* not have noticed?

'Amy!' Gina protested. 'I bumped into her today. She had your hairdo, your jeans, your jacket, your boots . . . in fact I thought it was you.'

'Nah . . .' Amy shrugged, feeling embarrassed.

'Do you know what she was doing?' Gina went on. 'She was in the Modern Art Gallery shop buying a poster that's exactly the same as the one you've got hanging above your bed. That's a little extreme, isn't it?'

'Well . . . yeah – that is taking things a bit far,' Amy had to agree, but she didn't seem nearly as het up about it as Gina was on her behalf. 'I'm not sure what to do,' she admitted. 'She's nice. I don't want to hurt her feelings.'

'She's trying to turn herself into *you*!' Gina insisted. 'Don't you think that's just a little spooky? Maybe she's thinking about going after Jason. And has it never occurred to you that your biggest fan is maybe the one who's got your necklace?'

'*Rosie?*' Amy exclaimed. 'She would never do anything like that. She knows just how much Jason and that necklace mean to me!'

'Well, have you asked her about him?' Gina demanded. 'And have you even told her your necklace is missing?'

'Gina! There are posters up – the whole boarding house knows it's missing! But you're totally wrong here,' Amy shot back, looking angry now. 'I know Rosie. She's been really nice to me about Jason when no one else seemed very interested. She wouldn't dream of taking my things. In fact, why don't you come with me?' She headed for the door. 'Come on!' she urged.

Gina got up from the sofa and reluctantly followed

195

her friend out of the room. Together they hurried down the corridor towards Rosie's dorm.

'You're not going to be able to talk to her now,' Gina pointed out to Amy. 'I think she's still in town.'

'I don't want to talk to her, I want you to look through her drawers with me and accept that you are completely wrong.'

'I'm not doing that!' Gina said, appalled. Hadn't looking through Penny's locker caused quite enough trouble? Penny now glared at them in every lesson and did everything she could to cause trouble for them at school.

'Yes you are. You can't accuse someone of something as major as this and then not follow it through. Anyway, Rosie borrowed a top of mine last week. I'll just tell her I urgently needed it back, so I had to go in and get it.'

'Amy, no!' Gina insisted.

But Amy was not going to be stopped.

The door of Rosie's dorm was already open. Then the door of Rosie's bedside cabinet was open and Amy was rootling around in it.

Out came the expensive Clarins hand cream that Amy used, a make-up bag – which on quick inspection was filled with Mac, Amy's favourite brand – then a pink leather diary with a lock on the front. A small photo album was next. When Amy flipped through it, she was taken aback to find it contained only photos of her and Rosie taken in Dubai. Then she brought out a small half-used bottle of pink nail varnish that she recognized as hers. Next a small tortoiseshell comb that she had been missing for a week or two.

'Both of those belong to you!' Gina said, remembering Amy's search for the items.

'OK, it's a little bit strange,' Amy had to agree. 'But maybe I lent them to her and I've just forgotten . . .'

But then a tan-coloured fishnet knee-high came out of the cabinet. Amy just *knew* it was hers. She remembered it had a little hole in the toe and she'd thrown it in the bin.

'Euwww,' Gina remarked when Amy placed the pop sock on the bed, beside the comb and the nail varnish. 'Please don't tell me that's yours as well? She's making a voodoo doll of you. That's what she's doing!'

Amy scooped up a pile of papers lying at the bottom of the cabinet, and as she did so, a small crumpled black and white photo cut from a school magazine slid out and fell between her fingers to the floor.

She didn't need to look to know who it was. With a

sinking feeling, she picked up the stamp-sized photo and saw that of course it was Jason.

'Oh, *mince*!' she exclaimed, giving Gina a flash of the photo, then began to pack Rosie's belongings quickly back into the locker. She scooped up the 'misplaced' items that belonged to her and told Gina, 'That's enough. I'm not looking through anything else. I'll talk to her – I'll just have to talk to her.'

When they were back on the stairs, Gina wondered aloud where Min was – she hadn't seen her since breakfast.

'In the study,' Amy sighed. 'She's always in the study now. Last year was bad, but this year is completely ridiculous. She never comes out of there.'

Gina felt a pang of guilt that she had still not told Amy anything about Min's cyber friend – but she had promised Min she wouldn't.

'Let's go and get her,' she decided. 'Maybe *she*'ll know what to do about Rosie.'

'Oh, God!' Amy grimaced. 'This is *so* embarrassing. A Year Four girl has got a crush on my crush and a crush on me! There's no other word for it, is there?'

Gina had to stifle a giggle at this.

Min was so absorbed by what she was doing at one of the study room computers that she didn't hear her friends come in.

Only when Gina was right next to her, whispering, 'Hello, Min! Stop working! Take a break! It's Sunday!' did she look up with a start.

'Oh! Hello! I didn't expect to—' Hurriedly, she flicked her mouse across her desk and closed down the page she'd been looking at.

'It's OK, Min,' Amy assured her. 'We're not going to copy your physics homework, no matter how amazing it is.'

'No, it's . . . um . . .' Min looked flustered; Gina realized immediately that she had been emailing the Gecko again.

'Relax!' Amy assured her. 'We were just missing you, and there's something I want to ask your advice about.'

When Min had been told all about Rosie and the hairstyle, the gallery poster, the nail varnish, the comb and the spooky knee-high, she leaned back in her chair and told Amy that there was only one thing she could do: 'You'll have to stage an intervention.'

'A *what*?' Amy was confused.

'You'll just have to go and face her – and ask her all about this. Take one of us, if you like. And you should definitely ask her about the necklace too,' Min advised. 'She might know something.'

Supper was long over and it was almost time for the youngest boarders to go up to their dorms when Amy finally decided to go and look for Rosie.

But first she went in search of Gina; after looking in the dorm and the common room, she finally found her in the study.

'Hi!' Amy went up to her and whispered, 'Why are you working on a Sunday night?'

'Oh, I'm not really,' Gina said, and pushed the pages of her play under a textbook. She still wasn't totally happy with it, she still didn't know if she was going to enter the competition or not and she *definitely* didn't want anyone to find out about it.

'Will you come with me to see Rosie?' Amy asked her. 'I just have a feeling this isn't going to be very easy.'

'Sure.' Gina was happy to agree because, if she was honest, a little part of her maybe, very selfishly, wanted Amy to fall out with Rosie.

They made their way down the corridor towards the Year Four sitting room, where they were sure Rosie would be: weekend evenings, free of homework, were currently a frenzy of creative activity as girls busied themselves making costumes for the Halloween party.

What had begun as a suggestion by Gina had taken life and shape and was now a major and eagerly anticipated event in the boarding-house calendar. Gina, who was on the organizing team, had already planned a weird and wonderful menu of food and drink. A disco had been booked, *boys* had been invited, and now the spooky, ghoulish dress code had to be obeyed. No one not in a Halloween costume was going to be allowed in and that was final.

So now girls who'd never before had a needle and thread in their hands were busy in their sitting rooms with black felt, sequins, sparkles and feathers, trying to create outfits that were scary but nevertheless flatteringly cute.

But before Amy and Gina could reach the sitting-room door, it was flung open by three of Rosie's friends, who all looked frightened.

'What's the matter?' Amy asked.

'There's a man!' one of the girls shrieked. 'There's a man in the garden!'

'He looked in at the window!' a second girl added, not quite so upset now that she was out in the corridor.

'It gave us a horrible fright,' the third girl said, visibly shaken.

There were now other girls in the corridor who had heard the screams and hurried out of the study and the other sitting rooms.

One of the sixth formers stepped forward to take charge. 'Is he still there?' she asked the girls.

'I don't know – we just ran out of the room.'

'Come on,' the older girl briskly instructed two of her friends. 'Let's tell Mrs K and go and find out what's happening.'

Amy and Gina ran after the group of girls heading for the front door.

'There's a man in the gardens!' one of the sixth formers called out to the Neb as she came out of her sitting room to see what was going on. 'We're going out to have a look,' the girl went on.

'A man in the gardens?' the Neb repeated; then, having digested the news, she started issuing brisk instructions of her own. 'No!' she barked at once. 'No one's going into the gardens without me! Katie, you dial 999 and alert the police! We can't have intruders lurking about the grounds.'

The housemistress went back into her sitting room and came out armed with a large golfing umbrella. Then, followed by a posse of girls, she threw open the front door and stepped out.

It was dark outside, velvety black. There was a streetlight but it was more than a hundred metres away from the house, beyond the large garden.

'Follow me and we'll do a clockwise tour right round the grounds. Follow me!' Mrs Knebworth barked again. 'We can't have people wandering off on their own. We must stick together.'

Through the dark garden they went, but it was empty. If someone had been there, then they had now well and truly gone.

'Where was he spotted?' Mrs Knebworth asked.

'Outside the Year Four common room,' came the reply.

'Let's take a look,' she commanded.

Beneath the common-room window was the proof that the three girls in the room had not been mistaken. In the newly dug earth was a clear footprint.

Caitlin, one of the Sixth Formers, had had the presence of mind to bring out a little pocket torch and she shone it down onto the earth. 'It's a big footprint,' she commented. 'Definitely a guy's.'

'Looks like a trainer,' someone else said, bending down to get a closer look.

'So he could sneak in quietly, then run away

quickly,' the Neb concluded. 'The coward!' she added fiercely.

Not one of the girls doubted that if the prowler were to suddenly appear in the garden before them, Mrs K would knock him down with her golfing umbrella, which was very comforting. There was no need to be nervous when the boarding house and all its inhabitants were protected by a fearsome Edinburgh battleaxe like their housemistress.

Just then they heard a car pulling into the driveway and saw the flash of blue lights on the grass. The police had arrived on the other side of the building.

'OK – inside, everyone,' Mrs Knebworth instructed them. 'I'd better take the officers to the scene of the crime. Upper Fifths!' she added. 'It's after nine thirty – straight upstairs to your dorms.'

Back in the Iris dorm, Amy had to let Min and Gina know what bad news the prowler was.

'It's not just that it's creepy having some guy wandering around looking in the windows,' she began, turning her back to them as she undressed. 'Don't be surprised if the Neb really does her nut about it. What I'm worried about is if she now thinks she has an excuse to cancel the party—'

Just then there came a sharp rap at the door.

'Here she is,' Amy hissed. 'Come to give us our goodnight kiss.'

The door opened with a slow creak and then the housemistress came into the room.

The Neb got straight to the point of her visit. 'If anyone knows anything about the person who was in the grounds this evening, they'd better come and tell me as soon as possible. Any delay will just make things much worse. The police are involved, so if anyone has even a suspicion, they'd better come to me as soon as possible.'

She added the most crucial, not to mention devastating, bit of information almost as an after-thought: 'After all this, I can't allow boys to come to the Halloween party. We'll just have to make our own fun.'

Chapter Twenty-three

Mrs Parker was sitting on her table in front of the class. She'd perched her reading glasses on her nose and seemed to be looking though the papers scattered across the top of the desk for something in particular.

'OK . . . time to stop writing, girls,' she announced. 'I'd like you to finish off whatever you've not managed in class as your homework for tonight. Now, there are just a few minutes before the bell, so I wanted to make an early announcement about the drama competition.'

Several expectant faces looked up quickly.

'The four plays have been chosen from the ninety-five entries we received from girls right through the senior school. Mrs Bannerman will announce the winners at assembly tomorrow – those whose plays will be performed by each house – but I just thought you might like to know that one of them is by someone in this class.' Mrs Parker smiled at the group in front of her.

'Oh no!' Amy whispered under her breath at Gina. 'What are we going to do? Are we going to tell her that Penny's been cheating?'

Gina was gripping the pen in her hand so tightly that her knuckles had turned white.

'Don't worry, you don't have to—' Amy began, but she was interrupted by Miss Parker's announcement:

'Gina Peterson, well done! Your one-act play, *Seeing Scarlett*, was an absolute delight.'

As applause broke out in the class, both Gina and Amy looked at one another in astonishment. Amy was totally amazed that Gina had never even mentioned she was entering. Gina just couldn't believe that all her secret hard work completed in the study room stints after her homework had paid off.

'That's brilliant!' Min told her. 'I wondered why you were spending almost as much time in the study as me.'

'You *are* a dark horse, Gina Peterson,' Amy teased.

'Penny?' Mrs Parker was asking, and Amy and Gina glanced quickly at one another. Had the B-H really dared hand in her copied play? 'I was surprised you didn't enter,' the teacher went on. 'I'd have thought you'd have come up with something good.'

Penny glared furiously in Amy and Gina's direction before replying: 'Well . . . I tried but I just couldn't come up with something really . . .'

'Original?' Amy chipped in.

In the afternoon Amy spotted Rosie in the dining room in a little huddle of Year Fours.

For half an hour after school, the dining room and part of the kitchen were opened up to the boarders so they could make themselves enough toast and tea to keep them going until supper at six thirty.

'Rosie?' Amy began.

'Hi, Amy, how are you?'

Amy saw the happy, smiling face turned in her direction and suddenly she had no idea where to begin the conversation about stolen pop socks and copy-cat outfits and secret photos of Jason.

'Fine, fine,' Amy answered. 'I just wondered if . . .' Well, she would at least mention the necklace again, she decided. If Rosie was hiding it, she wanted to prick her conscience. 'If you'd had any more bright ideas about finding my necklace. It's still missing and I'm really upset about it. My dad is going to have a fit.'

Rosie patted the bench beside her and urged Amy

to sit down so they could both have a think about it. 'Have you heard the prowler latest?' she added. 'It's good news and bad.'

'Oh, God,' Amy groaned. 'What new ways to make our lives miserable has the Neb come up with now?'

'Everyone not coming back to the boarding house straight after school has to come back in a group of three,' Rosie said.

'But what if you're the only boarder?'

'You have to arrange for a group to come over and get you,' Rosie explained.

'You're joking!'

'And we all have to carry torches and she's even thinking about rape alarms!'

'Why not just kit us out with mace! Does this prowler even exist?' Amy wanted to know. 'Is there any proof that they weren't just seeing . . . I dunno . . . Mel searching through the bushes for her lost knickers or something.'

'The police have taken details of the footprint. It was a size ten trainer, apparently,' one of Rosie's friends added.

'What's the good news then?' Amy wondered. 'What possible good can have come of this?'

'Well, there *is* hope,' Rosie assured her. 'Someone

has suggested a male guest list at the door for the Halloween party—'

'Yesss!' Amy broke in.

'Hand-selected, Mrs K-approved names only,' Rosie said. 'A list that she can tick off, to make sure that only the "nice young men" from St Lennox and the like are allowed in. Apparently she's thinking about it.'

'I have to go.' Amy sprang to her feet. 'I have to email Jason!'

'Jason?' Rosie exclaimed. 'Do you think he will come?'

It was the excitement in Rosie's voice that suddenly filled Amy with a surge of anger.

'Look,' she said quietly but firmly, right up against Rosie's ear. 'If Jason is going to go out with anyone at St Jude's, then it is going to be me. Not you or anyone else, just me. And,' she went on, deciding that now she'd started, she might as well get it all off her chest, 'I can't believe that you've bought exactly the same jacket as me, the same jeans, even the same flaming handbag! You've got *my* poster above your bed, you're wearing your hair in *my* kind of ponytail and you've even got exactly the same hairclip! You are a total copycat, Rosie! An ID thief!'

At this Rosie burst into tears and ran out of the dining room.

Chapter Twenty-four

Amy was in town, in one of her favourite shopping streets, *alone*. She couldn't believe she had managed it!

It was all because she'd originally ordered her special Halloween costume from this fancy dress company in London. She'd been all set to hire this amazing ghostly ball dress from *Phantom of the Opera*. But then, yesterday, she'd opened up an email informing her that 'due to unforeseen circumstances . . . etc., etc.' The costume wasn't just delayed; it wasn't coming at all!

After going to Mrs Knebworth in a state of distress, she pleaded to be allowed into town on her own this Saturday morning because every single one of her friends was too busy with party or costume preparation and she had to go and get something or she really would have absolutely *nothing* to wear . . .

Once the bus pulled to a halt in George Street, she

bounced happily down the steps and out onto the pavement.

George Street was long and broad, with beautiful grey stone buildings. Its shops were of the chic and expensive kind. Perfume, old-fashioned stationery, high fashion, luxury bags – these were the items for sale here. At the far end of the street was St Andrew's Square and the high temple of girl shopping: the northern outpost of the fashion department store, Harvey Nichols.

Despite their recent disagreements about Jason and Gary, there was one thing on which Amy and her dad could agree: Amy's generous allowance. Amy got more pocket money per month than any other girl she knew at St Jude's. Even though she had now broken the news about her lost diamond necklace to her dad and had listened to his agitated lecture about money and how it 'didn't grow on trees', she knew that there was still a very comfortable amount in her bank account today.

As she went through the department store's rotating glass doors, Amy surveyed the beauty and make-up counters in front of her. Well, it wouldn't hurt to wander around here for a while before she rode the escalators upstairs and had a look through the amazing dresses for something just Halloweenish enough to get away with.

It was as she was applying a third, ever so slightly different shade of lip gloss that Amy caught sight of someone reflected in the mirror behind her.

The person quickly dipped back behind a column and she thought she must have imagined it. But she put the lid back on the gloss, turned on her heel and walked quickly over to the column.

There was no one there. But as she looked about her, she caught a fleeting glimpse of copper leather jacket. With a flash of anger, Amy began to march in the jacket's direction. Rounding the corner, she walked straight up to Rosie, grabbed hold of her arm and demanded, 'What are you doing here? Are you now *following* me?'

A rush of emotions played across Rosie's face: shock, embarrassment, regret.

'What are you doing?' Amy repeated. When Rosie just shook her head nervously, she asked, 'Are you here on your own?'

'Yes,' Rosie replied.

'How did you get permission?' Amy demanded.

'I said . . . erm, I said I was going with you,' Rosie said timidly.

Amy let go of Rosie's copper-brown leather jacket, which was just like her own; she looked at Rosie's jeans, the same brand as hers; Rosie's boots, again the same; Rosie's ponytail, just what Amy had chosen today; even Rosie's dinky little shoulder bag was Marc by Marc Jacobs, *exactly* the same pricey and unusual choice as Amy's.

'Couldn't you at least have tried to stop copying me!' Amy burst out. 'And now you're spying on me! You've got to stop it! Look at you, you're like my clone! This is ridiculous! Please stop! People at school are laughing at us!'

Rosie flushed a deep red with embarrassment and Amy could see that tears were springing up in her eyes again.

'And stop crying!' she snapped.

'I didn't mean to copy—' Rosie began.

'Yes you did!' Amy exclaimed. 'You're wearing all these things on purpose! You came here on purpose!'

'I just wanted one or two things *like* yours . . .' Rosie began. 'And . . . I don't know, I got a bit carried away. I didn't think you'd mind,' she added in a very quiet voice, then looked down at her feet and started to sob. Right there in the Mulberry handbag concession! Oh, good grief, this was so embarrassing. Amy looked around and saw heads turning in their direction.

'Go away,' Rosie blurted out, wiping a hand across her face. 'Please go away!'

For a moment Amy was tempted to do just that – turn and walk away as quickly as she could.

'Just leave me alone!' Rosie insisted, her face still in her hands.

But then Amy remembered all the time Rosie had spent listening to her Jason sorrows. Rosie had only wanted to be nice; had only wanted to be her friend!

So instead, feeling a pang of regret, Amy went and put an arm round Rosie's shoulder.

'You have my old pop sock in your bedside cabinet,' she said, but with a hint of kindly meant teasing.

'Oh no!' Rosie spluttered in astonishment, trying to pull away. 'I didn't want you to know about that!'

'I think you've gone off your trolley,' Amy soothed, 'but it's OK. I'm flattered really – you're my very first stalker . . .'

Rosie began to sob freely now, so Amy pulled her towards one of the make-up counters, where she'd spotted a box of tissues.

'Shhhhh . . .' She tried to calm the younger girl. 'You'll get me banned from Harvey Nicks and then my life just won't be worth living. It's all right,' she insisted. 'Everyone does daft things – I know I've done—'

Amy broke off mid-sentence, because she'd now seen something really worrying. She ducked down behind the make-up counter mirror, but then couldn't resist taking a furtive little peek.

Was that Jason? Had he just walked in through the front door . . . with another girl?

Amy put her hand on Rosie's arm and ushered her quickly round the corner at the foot of the escalators so they wouldn't be spotted.

'What's the matter?' Rosie asked, realizing that something other than having a devoted fan was on Amy's mind.

'Shhh – tell you in a minute,' Amy whispered. She was too busy trying to take sneak peeks at her supposed 'boyfriend' and the girl he was with to be able to give a full explanation right now.

She'd seen this girl before – the tall, enviably lovely-looking one. It was the gazelle, wasn't it? It was the girl he'd kissed on the cheeks that day at the café. Well, here he was all cosied up with her. Look! They were holding hands and he was guiding her upstairs. On the escalator, he slid his hand into her back pocket and he must have squeezed her bum because she gave a little shriek.

Amy quickly turned away and hid behind a hand-bag display.

They were probably going up to the top floor together to sip cappuccinos while gazing into each other's eyes, she thought. Or maybe they were going to wander through the racks of clothes, picking out lovely things for each other to wear on all their many future dates . . .

'What's the matter?' Rosie asked with concern. 'You look like you've seen a ghost.'

'Yeah!' Amy replied bitterly, feeling a lump at the back of her throat. 'The ghost of my supposed relationship.'

'That was Jason, wasn't it?' Rosie asked next.

'Yeah.'

'He's so good looking,' Rosie told her admiringly. 'Who was that g—?'

Before Rosie could finish her question, Amy said emphatically, 'Yeah, soooo good looking, but such an arse.'

'Are you OK?' Rosie wondered.

'I'm fine, I'm going to be fine,' Amy replied, trying to pull herself together. 'How about you?'

'Yeah – not too bad.'

'I'd suggest a coffee, but I really need to get out of here and I still have to get something to wear to the party tonight. Shall we go somewhere else?' Amy offered with a smile.

Rosie smiled back. 'Yeah,' she agreed.

'C'mon then, stalker,' Amy added – well, she couldn't resist.

It was 2.15 when they walked into the Arts Café, Amy weighed down with the bulging bag containing her costume. She hadn't heard a word from Jason, so if he was still going to show up for their date, she wanted to make sure he'd have a nice long wait for her, so she was a full thirty minutes late.

Sweeping her eyes around the busy room, she could see Gina, she could see Min, both waving in her direction. She could see Dermot rushing towards a table with a tray full of drinks. But no sign of Jason.

If Jason had been here, well, then, there might have been a chance that the gazelle wasn't anyone important. That maybe she was a friend – or his best friend's sister, or— Ha! Who was she trying to kid?

Jason wasn't here because he was with the gazelle. You'd have to be a complete idiot not to work that out. And Amy was not an idiot. Definitely not.

'Hi, Gina! Hi, Min.' Amy stuck her most cheerful smile onto her face and walked over towards their table.

'You're so late,' Gina complained. 'We'll have to go in about five minutes to get everything ready. Wait till you see my bugs!' she added.

'Hi, Rosie!' Min said, surprised that Amy had come with her Year Four friend.

'What bugs?' Rosie asked, settling into a chair.

Gina delved in her handbag and brought out a small plastic tub. She lifted the lid and, to Rosie and Amy's horror, revealed a selection of dead insects: fat black beetles, a gangly-legged spider, a centipede.

'Eeuww!' Rosie exclaimed, jerking back from the tub.

'They're not real,' Min explained. 'Gina spotted them in this deli.'

'Liquorice,' Gina confirmed. 'So I'm not eating one, but I thought we could decorate the food with them – have a beetle or two in the slime soup.'

'Disgusting . . . but brilliant,' Amy had to admit.

'So where is Jason?' Gina asked, putting her tub away. 'He's not coming then?'

'Jason who?' Amy asked, pulling up a chair. 'Forget it!'

Just then Dermot appeared at her elbow. 'Jason?' he repeated. 'Uh-oh. Invasion of the posh boys due to happen any minute now then, is it? I'd better put on my flat cap so I can bow and doff it at them properly.'

'Oh, very funny,' Gina told him.

'Is he still coming to the Halloween party tonight?' Min asked Amy, wondering why Gina was pulling such a horrified face.

'Not if I can help it.' Amy was desperate to talk about something else. 'You've got to see Rosie's new bag,' she enthused. 'It's gorgeous! I helped her pick it out and it's subtly different from mine!' she teased lightly. 'Then there's my costume for the Halloween party, which is totally fantastic!' She pulled her shopping bag up onto her lap.

'Halloween party?' Dermot was craning over Amy for a little more information now. 'Party?' He looked at Gina. 'At your school?'

'Yeah,' Amy answered. 'At the boarding house. Gina's one of the organizers. Gina, you said you'd invited Dermot,' she added, not realizing what a blunder she'd just made.

Gina began to fiddle nervously with her hair and everyone noticed the unhappy colouring of her cheeks. 'Umm, well . . . yeah, but . . .' she began. How the hell was she going to explain this?

Since their art gallery date, Gina had been playing it cool again. She'd told Dermot that she was too busy this weekend and had only offered to 'pop into' the café to say hello. It wasn't just the Scarlett note in the diary that had made her decide not to invite Dermot to the Halloween party; it was also because – due to the 'prowler' – Mrs Knebworth was policing the invitation list like a jailer: every boy invited was listed by age and school. It wouldn't have surprised Gina if they'd had to bring their birth certificates to the door to get in.

But Gina hadn't wanted to put Dermot's name down on that list. She knew he would be the only boy not from one of the private schools and she felt embarrassed about it. The Neb was bound to raise her eyebrows, sniff and ask lots of nosy questions.

Nor did she want to make him feel awkward. She didn't want the Neb interviewing him; she didn't want the other snooty boys at the party looking down their noses at him either. Plus, she was going to have to ask him about Scarlett before she could ever kiss him or go on a date with him again. She was going to *have* to. No matter how scared she was of hearing the answer.

221

'Yeah but *what*?' Dermot asked Gina bluntly. 'Yeah but unfortunately I'm not from St Snooty's and I don't have a dinner jacket hanging in the cupboard, so why even bother asking me? Is that how it is?'

'No!' Gina protested.

'It's fancy dress, anyway,' Amy broke in.

'Oh well, I could have come to that, no problem, Gina!' Dermot insisted angrily. 'I could just have come as myself and everyone would have been totally horrified!'

A very uncomfortable feeling was building up in Gina. Everyone seemed to be looking at her; everyone seemed to be blaming her. No one knew the other reason – the real reason why Gina just couldn't relax and enjoy Dermot's company; couldn't yet treat him like a real boyfriend.

'I know all about Scarlett,' she exclaimed, feeling her heart hammer in her chest. 'I *know*, Dermot.'

'*What*?' He sounded utterly astonished.

Gina was on her feet; with shaking hands she was scrambling for her bag and her jacket. She just wanted to get out of here. This was the most embarrassing situation she'd ever, *ever* found herself in. Dermot's dad was coming out from behind the counter; in a moment he was going to tell them all off. Min, Amy and Rosie were all looking at Gina in complete astonishment.

'But what's that got to do with anything?' Dermot called after Gina.

'I think we should just get out of here,' Amy told her friends. They all began to collect their things together so they could follow Gina out.

'And if you see Jason,' Amy aimed at Dermot, 'can you just tell him that boys are a big fat waste of time?'

The moment they walked in the front door, Mrs Knebworth spotted Amy and called out to her.

'In my sitting room, Miss McCorquodale. I've a surprise for you.'

'Oh, brother,' Amy said in a low voice. The Neb's surprises were never usually good ones. *What have I done now?* she wondered.

The upright piano in Mrs Knebworth's sitting room was overwhelmed by a stunning bunch of pink flowers. Fat pink peonies, deep pink roses, luscious heads of sweet William, all beautifully wrapped in cellophane and tied with a broad satin ribbon.

'Those are gorgeous.' Amy pointed at the flowers, hoping to soften up the Neb for whatever was coming.

Perhaps she was going to ask her to dress up as a pumpkin and greet people at the door?

'Aren't they just?' the housemistress agreed. 'I've taken the liberty of putting them in a vase. I hope you don't mind.'

'*I* don't mind?' Amy asked in confusion. 'Why would *I* mind?'

'They're for you, Amy.' The Neb gave Amy a rare smile. 'And it's not even your birthday! Lucky girl. There's a card.'

Amy couldn't believe it. Why would her dad send her flowers? Flowers just weren't really his thing. Diamonds, yes; flowers, no.

'Flowers?' Amy murmured in confusion as her friends crowded into the room behind her, eager to take a look at the blooms, not to mention the card.

She tore open the little envelope and read the words: *So sorry to miss you. Got called to match at short notice. Will see you tonight. Jason xx.*

She closed the card and stuffed it quickly back into its envelope. This was just the final straw. He didn't call. He didn't show up. But he still sent extravagant bunches of flowers! He just didn't have a clue! He was so confusing, she just didn't think she could take any more.

This was the second time Jason had sent flowers. The first time, last term, it had been incredible. But this time it felt like a stunt.

'They look really nice in here,' Amy told Mrs K. 'I think we'll just leave them where they are.'

Chapter Twenty-five

As the party was due to start at seven thirty, by seven there was noisy, crowded chaos in the boarding-house dorms. Black netting and black maribou trims were unravelling, spider-web fishnets were ripping, witchy black and silver corsets were coming unhooked, black and purple hairspray cans were misfiring and causing all sorts of unexpected problems.

In the Iris dorm, Amy and Gina were surveying their costumes with a degree of contentment. Amy was a cute black cat in a long-sleeved cat suit and a headband with little black ears attached. Gina was wearing a witch's hat, a leotard and a short black tutu. Then she'd added black leggings so as not to give Mrs Knebworth palpitations.

Amy went to her chest of drawers and brought out a plastic box of her own. 'Do you want to see *my* bugs?' she asked Gina with a mischievous smile, and lifted the lid.

Inside was a small collection of very *real* insects: two spiders, one still moving, three black beetles, legs wiggling, and a moth.

'Eeek!' was Gina's reaction.

'I thought I'd try and create some fun. I mean, Dermot isn't coming, and if Jason turns up, I'll have to listen to a load of lies and excuses. So let's see who we can get to eat a real bug instead of a liquorice one.'

'Yuck! That is mean, Amy,' was Gina's verdict.

'C'mon, if I got Jason to accidentally eat crunchy Mr Beetle here, you'd laugh, wouldn't you?'

'Well . . . if it's Jason we're talking about—'

Just then the dorm door opened and in came Min. She'd been in the bathroom for some time and now the girls knew why.

Min – who had never, to anyone's knowledge, been interested in boys and had never had a boyfriend – slipped in with a shy smile, looking like the foxiest version of Morticia Addams ever.

Her slinky black dress had a slashed neckline and a side split that travelled all the way up to mid thigh. Her blue-black hair had been left loose, and the deep purple lipstick and black eyeliner made her look really grown up and gorgeous. But the mysterious thing was that she was fizzing with some sort of secret happiness; it kept bursting out with little giggles and smiles.

'What are you so pleased about?' Amy had to ask. 'Well, apart from the fact that you are going to be the most fabulous girl at the entire party.'

'Nothing!' Min insisted, but let out another giggle.

'You've got a crush, haven't you?' Amy asked. 'I can't believe I've not noticed who it is!'

Then she and Gina began working down the list of boys they knew were coming, with Min screaming out horrified denials at every single one of the names.

That was when they were alerted to a beeping noise coming from Gina's mobile.

'How come you've got your phone?' Min asked.

'My mom's calling me later, so the Neb said it was OK.'

Gina went over to her chest of drawers and took the phone out. 'Sounds like she's sent me a text.' But she opened the message and saw that it wasn't from her mother.

The message read simply: SCARLETT IS A SHORT STORY. NOT A GIRL. DOES THAT HELP? D.

'Oh no!' Gina said, sitting down on the bed, not taking her eyes off the phone screen. 'Oh *no!*'

Before she would answer anyone's concerned

questions, she texted back the reply: I AM AN IDIOT. SO SORRY. G XX.

'Come on!' The shout came from outside their door. 'Time to go down and make sure everything's ready.'

Amy recognized the voice. 'That's Rosie. She said she was going as a frog! We've got to see her costume.'

Gina put the phone back into her drawer, then hurried out onto the landing, where Rosie was indeed dressed up as a frog, but a very cute green frog, complete with a tiara perched at an angle on her head.

'You know, I'm the frog princess: you kiss me and I turn out beautiful.'

'You're already beautiful!' Amy assured her.

'Look at you guys though – *whoa!*' was her reply.

Downstairs, the three common rooms given over to the party looked amazing. Large cobwebby nets had been draped over the doors and ceilings. Low green lamps gave off a ghoulish glow. Carved pumpkins lit with candles had been scattered around the garden and steps. Mrs K had insisted, due to fire regulations, there should be none indoors.

Gina had come up with most of the inspired suggestions for the Halloween buffet. There was dark spaghetti, slimy pea soup, vampish beetroot soup, and jugs full of the specially mixed blood-red soft drink. Liquorice bugs had been dotted all over the food and plates.

But Gina still couldn't hide her disappointment at the sweet selection. Yes, there were white chocolate mice and skulls, pumpkin lollies and chocolate balls wrapped in special pumpkin foil, but it just couldn't compete with a proper American Halloween candy spread. What she really wanted to see were jellied pumpkins, chocolate pumpkins, sweets shaped into witches, broomsticks, ghosts and little black cats, seasonally decorated Reese's Pieces made of delicious peanut butter covered in chocolate, and pumpkin pie! When she had suggested making pumpkin pie to Mrs K, she'd received a very blank look.

One of the eager girls who had been posted at a window now announced with a mixture of nerves and excitement, 'I think that's a minibus pulling up. I think the boys are here!'

The music was turned up loud, the disco lights began to whirl around the room and there were several long minutes of almost breathless anticipation while costumes were tweaked, eyeliner smudged, lip gloss quickly reapplied. Then, with slightly forced laughter and over-loud 'hellos', the first group of boys entered the room.

It was hard to tell who was who – there were so many guests here all of a sudden and their costumes were so weird and wonderful. There were wizards of course. Lots of blue and black bathrobes had been pressed into service. Then several ghoulish monks, Frankensteins, Draculas, and someone in one of those horrible black and white frozen *Scream* masks.

'Oh no!' Amy exclaimed. 'I hate those screaming skull things, they give me the creeps. Niffy and I watched that film one half-term and . . . it's just horrible!'

The skull began to approach them, and even though Amy knew it was just a mask, she could feel herself shrinking back.

'Hi!' the skull boomed, and they immediately recognized Angus's voice.

'Hello!' They greeted him enthusiastically.

'I didn't know you were coming,' Amy began. 'You should have told us – we'd have had something to look forward to.'

'Oh yeah! But I'm only here for the beer,' he joked.

'There isn't any,' Gina warned him; she was now being jostled by the crowd of new arrivals.

'Well, that's the good thing about baggy clothing.' He flapped his black arms about. 'It can hide a lot of bulging pockets.'

'You've brought booze!' Amy whispered excitedly – a few mouthfuls of beer and she had a feeling her nerves at seeing Jason tonight wouldn't be quite so bad.

'Yeah, in subtle cans, so from a distance it will look just like Coke.'

'Very clever,' Gina agreed.

As they scanned over the Draculas and assorted ghouls to see who else they recognized, Min said she had to go to the bathroom and made her way out of the room.

'She looks great,' Angus told the other girls.

'We know!' said Gina. 'We just have no idea who for.'

Then Amy saw the most dapper Dracula of all coming in and knew immediately who she was looking at.

Jason was in his dinner jacket with a white shirt and white bow tie. He'd not bothered with fake fangs or even much white face powder; he'd just attached a silky cloak to his shoulders and swept his hair back from his face in the hope that this would be enough.

'There he is,' Gina prompted. 'Do you want us to hide you?'

'No, no,' Amy insisted. 'I've eaten plenty of garlic.'

'Oh, very good,' Angus laughed. 'That should keep the vampires away!'

With quiet determination, Amy walked steadily across the dance floor, where several witches and a ghoul or two were bravely kicking off the dancing.

As soon as Jason spotted her, he held his arms out wide and gave a leery 'Hello, baby,' as his opening line.

Which was a mistake.

If Amy had been angry before, she was furious now. How dare he 'Hello, baby' her!

She walked straight past him and into the corridor, hoping he would follow. It was quieter out there and she wanted to make sure he heard her every word. He seemed to get the message and was soon out in the corridor beside her.

They weren't alone there. Small groups of girls and boys were mingling under the netting and the dangling spiders, but Amy came up close to Jason so that she could hiss in his ear.

'Did you send me those flowers?' she began furiously.

'Yeah!' Jason was smiling. 'I knew you'd love them.

They cost a fortune. What are you so annoyed about?'

'You were supposed to meet me this afternoon,' Amy went on.

'I know. I'm sorry, I got called into the team at short notice—'

She interrupted him with a sharp: 'Excuse me! Don't you own a mobile? Couldn't you have called me? Or sent a grovelling text? Were your fingers broken this afternoon?'

'I'm sorry, Amy!' he repeated. 'I couldn't find my phone and I couldn't get onto the payphone. I'm sorry.' And here he gave her such a charming smile and stretched out his hand to stroke her hair in such a tender manner that she might almost have relented and leaned up to kiss that shapely, ever so slightly arrogant pout if an image of the gazelle hadn't sprung up so clearly in her mind.

'We could have met in the morning. What were you doing earlier today that was so important?' she asked.

'Oh . . .' Dracula ran a hand over his slicked-back hair. 'There was someone I had to see.'

Oh yes, there certainly was, and Amy was going to find out all about it. 'Someone who?' she persisted.

'Just someone.' Jason shrugged his shoulders. 'It's not important – to do with school.'

'That is just bollocks and you know it,' Amy said, pointing a finger fiercely at his chest.

Jason had the sense to stay silent for a moment; he was trying to work out what was coming next.

'I saw you this morning. I saw you in Harvey Nichols with the tall blonde girl. You were holding her hand and squeezing her bum!' Amy added with as much outrage as she could muster. 'Out shopping, were you? Or taking her for a little treat up on the fourth floor? Buying *her* an ice cream, were you?'

Amy did not like the way her voice suddenly seemed to be cracking up over these words. She wished she was wearing a witch's hat so she could pull the brim down over her face and not let Jason see how upset she was.

What had happened to the person she had snuggled up to in her dad's nightclub all those weeks ago? Where *was* he?

Just face it, Amy – her dad's voice was ringing in her ears – *maybe he's just not that into you.*

'Oh here we go,' Jason began, but his voice sounded different. He didn't sound apologetic or kind or remotely lovely any more. He sounded just as angry as she was. 'You know, just because we've kissed and I've stayed the night at your flat doesn't mean you get to follow me around! I don't want a girlfriend and I definitely don't want a stalker,' he added. 'What's wrong with you and me hanging out and having fun when we can?'

'Fine!' Amy replied. 'That's fine! You just hang out and have your fun with that . . . that . . . spindly mop-body,' was the best she could come up with under pressure. 'Don't bother me! I'm not interested! And why don't you just collect your flowers on the way out? I don't bloody want them. Give them to mop-girl.'

With that she headed as quickly as she could towards the flight of stairs that led up to the bathrooms. Up there, behind a locked cubicle door . . . Well, pretty much everyone who came into the bathroom would be able to hear her cry.

Chapter Twenty-six

'Have you heard from Niffy recently?' Gina was shouting into Angus's ear, so as to be heard above the music.

'Yeah.' Angus smiled broadly at the mention of Niffy's name. 'Today was a really big day: her mum was seeing the consultant to get a fresh round of test results. I'm surprised she's not phoned,' he added. 'I tried to get hold of her before I came.'

'Oh!' Gina was surprised she didn't know about this development. Maybe Amy did, but hadn't mentioned it because she'd been so distracted by Jason.

'Do you think it's going to be bad news?' she asked.

'No idea.' Angus shook his head. 'Could be bad, could be good, could be no change.'

His friend Charlie Fotheringham was swaggering towards them in a cobbled-together Frankenstein costume. How appropriate, Gina couldn't help thinking: she'd always found him a bit of a monster.

'Hey there, Yankee,' he began, looking at Gina.

'Hello,' she answered coldly.

'Now apparently, Angus' – Charlie leaned over towards him – 'you are the man with the beers.'

'Indeed,' Angus confirmed, and ducked a hand under his loose black outfit into one of the deep pockets of his combat trousers underneath. Then he handed Charlie a small tin of supermarket own brand, carefully chosen because of the silver and red packaging which made it look, from a distance and in dim disco lighting, just like a Coke can.

'So' – Charlie turned to Gina again and gave her a big smile – 'where was your glamorous Asian babe friend headed?'

'Min?' Gina asked.

'Yes, the lovely Min. All she would tell me as she snuck out of the side door was to mind my own business.'

'The side door?' Gina didn't know what he meant. 'Which side door?'

'Well, I don't know – it looked as if it might lead into the back garden,' Charlie told her, 'but you're the one who lives here, aren't you?'

Lives *here*! Ha! She felt almost insulted by the suggestion. If only Charlie could see her real home, then maybe he'd stop being so rude and obnoxious to her. Actually, that made him even worse – the fact that his opinion of her would change once he knew about her wealthy background.

No sooner had she thought this than she suddenly felt a pang of shame. Hadn't her opinion of Dermot changed once she'd seen his home? That made her no better than Charlie, didn't it?

'So, are we going to dance then, Yankee?' Charlie asked, putting an unwelcome hand around her waist.

Gina quickly moved away from his touch. 'I'd love to,' she lied, 'but first you've got to tell me what you think of my slime soup.'

With a charming smile, she handed him the cup she'd been waiting to offer Jason.

'What the hell is that?' Charlie asked, peering at the insect floating on top of the green goo.

'Liquorice bugs,' Gina assured him. 'Aren't they cute?'

'Excellent!' Angus enthused, leaning in for a look. 'Snarf that down, Charlie, unless you want to give it to me.'

'Oi, back off,' Charlie told him, then fished the beetle out with his finger. Fortunately the hot soup seemed to have finished Amy's live beetle off;

otherwise his wriggling legs might have given the game away.

A moment later and the beetle was in Charlie's mouth. He chewed thoughtfully for a moment or two before saying, 'Just tastes of soup.'

'Excuse me a minute . . .' Gina had to turn away to hide her face; then, before she exploded with laughter, she rushed off to tell Amy.

The room was hot and very crowded now and she had to nudge and jostle past people to get to the door. *Scarlett was a short story!* This was almost all she could think about. Did she believe it? Had she gone and messed up everything with Dermot because she'd jumped to some stupid, jealous conclusion for no reason – other than the fact that she was just completely untrusting and insecure!

Why hadn't she just invited Dermot to this party? Then he'd be here and they'd have got talking and the whole Scarlett thing would probably have come out in conversation and she could have been laughing in relief with him. Hadn't she realized yet that he was the one and only great guy she'd met in Scotland and he was totally, *totally* into her, but she kept brushing him off and letting him down at every opportunity?

Gina pressed a finger to the corner of her eyes to try

to stem the tears that were forming there, and as she did so, she bumped straight into the soft foamy padding of some total idiot who had come to the party dressed up as a monstrous green Shrek.

'Sorry,' Shrek mumbled through his thick rubber mask. 'I can't see where I'm going.'

'No, my fault,' Gina assured him. 'I'm trying to get to the door.'

'Gina?' Shrek asked, to her surprise.

'Yes?' she answered, wondering who was in there.

With a large green hand, Shrek clumsily raised his face mask a little.

'Dermot?' Gina asked in astonishment.

'What am I doing here? I know . . .' Dermot began. 'And, more importantly, what am I doing here dressed like a big green idiot?' he joked.

'Dermot!' Gina repeated, still completely taken aback, but totally delighted to see him, even if he was dressed like a big green idiot.

'How did you get in?' she asked next. 'You can't have slipped past security looking like that!'

'That was the easy bit,' Dermot explained. 'I just followed some guys in and got ticked off a list. I think my name is now Olly Hughes, so make sure you call me that.'

'Why are you here, Olly?' was Gina's next question. The surprised delight at seeing him was wearing off rapidly and now all she could feel was embarrassed confusion.

'I came to say sorry . . .' Dermot lifted up his Shrek mask just a little further so that Gina could see his face. 'I'm a total prat,' he added. 'I think the American translation of that is a *jerk.*'

'No . . .' Gina put her hand on his arm. 'No, really, it's fine. It's me. I, erm . . . is Scarlett really a story?' she had to ask.

'Yes!' Dermot replied, sounding almost exasperated. 'How do you know about Scarlett, anyway?'

'Erm . . . looking through your computer files and seeing it in your diary.' Gina's eyes were fixed on the large green Shrek hand; she didn't want to look into his rubbery face.

'That's quite impressive,' Shrek said finally. 'I feel as if I've been fully vetted. Do you want to phone my English teacher and ask him about the story I'm writing for my course? He knows what it's called.'

'Er, no, I think that'll be OK.'

'Well, we are quite a pair, aren't we?' Shrek asked. 'The jealous lady and the super-sensitive tramp.'

Gina didn't know what to say; she just slipped her

hand into Shrek's and felt a happy and relieved smile flit across her face.

'Would you accept a peace offering?' Dermot said loudly against her ear, because the song currently belting from the sound system was making it hard to be heard.

'Yes!' Gina told him, wondering what was coming next.

He reached for the brown messenger bag that hung from his shoulder and opened up the flap. 'Look what I've made for you . . .' He held the bag open for Gina to see.

There was only a dim light in the room and they were both still being jostled by the crowd, but Gina could see something large and round carefully wrapped up with silver foil. But it was the smell from the bag that told her straight away what was in there.

'Pumpkin pie!' she exclaimed. 'You've made me a pumpkin pie? Dermot!'

'Olly,' he corrected her.

'How did you . . .? Where did you . . .? What made you . . .?' she began.

He was smiling broadly, very, very pleased with the success of his peace offering.

Gina stretched up, peeled back part of his mask and

kissed him on the cheek. 'You're great!' she told him, right into his ear. 'You are totally great. I'm sorry.'

Dermot put a large green hand on her waist. 'I think we should boogie,' he said.

'No! Not until I get a piece of pie!' she insisted. 'Where in the hell did you get the outfit anyway?' she wondered.

'Ah . . . well, we did this promotion at the café once. Look, just be grateful I didn't come as the donkey,' Dermot added.

Gina put her arm around him – well, she tried to but the foam rubber padding was so thick she couldn't reach all the way.

'Let's go find a knife and a plate and then we'll boogie,' she promised.

They began to push their way towards the door when Gina spotted Amy striding into the room with a look of fury written right across her face.

Chapter Twenty-seven

'What's wrong?' Gina asked Amy, just as soon as she and Dermot had made it through the pack of ghoulishly disguised bodies.

'Jason's left. He went into the Neb's study and had the nerve to take his flowers with him! I can't believe it! My dad was so right . . .'

Amy's face looked a little strange. It was pale and blotchy, as if she had been crying but had then used face powder to try and cover it up.

'I'm so sorry.' Gina took her hand from round Dermot's waist so that she could at least give Amy a sympathetic pat.

'You're with the jolly green giant,' Amy exclaimed, noticing for the first time that Gina was actually with the person swathed in green foam rubber. 'Who's in there?'

'Dermot,' Gina told her. 'But just for tonight he's going by the name of Olly Hughes.'

'Or Shrek, to his really close friends,' Amy couldn't help adding.

'Hello,' Dermot said. With his horrible green mask back in place, he gave a small theatrical bow in Amy's direction. 'You're a funky cat,' he added. 'But where's Min?' he asked them. 'I've not seen her costume yet.'

'Min!' Gina remembered all of a sudden. *Min!*

Hadn't Charlie said she'd gone out into the garden? Gina, distracted by Dermot, hadn't thought to ask anyone else if they'd seen her.

'What's the problem? She'll be around here some-where,' Amy said.

'No!' Gina began to feel strangely agitated. 'She's been really weird all evening. As if she's hiding some-thing from us; as if she's got some sort of special secret from us . . . and Charlie said she'd gone out into the garden, which is totally weird. Why would she go into the garden? Amy, I just know we should look for her – *now.*'

'This is *Min* we're talking about!' Amy broke in. 'Super-sensible, swotty Min. I'm going to look around this room,' she added calmly. 'You're going to look upstairs in the bathroom and our dorm, and Dermot's going to look in the corridor and the other party rooms. If we still can't find her, then we'll think about worrying. OK?'

It was a really sensible suggestion, so Gina quickly ran out of the room and up the stairs to carry out her part of the search.

Five minutes later the three of them met up again at the bottom of the stairs to admit that they'd drawn a blank.

'I can't believe this!' Gina said, now seriously worried. 'Something's not right.'

'Calm down,' Amy insisted.

'But did you ask people? Has anyone seen her?'

'No one I've spoken to has seen her since the party began,' Amy had to admit.

It was time for Gina to tell Amy about Min's secret. Yes, she'd made a promise not to, but she would worry about breaking her promise just as soon as they'd found Min safe and sound.

'Amy, there's something you don't know,' Gina began. 'Min has this guy she talks to on the Internet—'

As she registered both Amy and Dermot's shocked looks, she cursed herself for keeping all this to herself for so long.

'You are kidding . . .' Amy said slowly, immediately

understanding the seriousness of the situation now. 'Has she met him before?'

'No,' Gina answered, 'but she told me she was thinking about meeting him. I warned her to do it in a public place and to take one of us along, but do you think she might have gone out to meet him tonight?'

'Min?' Amy asked incredulously. 'Min? I don't know if she's even shaken hands with a boy before. This *can't* be happening.'

'It doesn't sound good,' Dermot added.

Already, without discussing it, the three of them were heading towards the back door of the boarding house.

'Do you think we should tell the Neb?' Gina wondered.

'No,' Amy said firmly. 'No need to make things worse than they already are. If we just cut through here' – she pointed to a door into the kitchen that Gina had never noticed before – 'we'll be able to reach the back door without too many people noticing.'

'You know,' Dermot began, 'I've never been to the boarding house before and I got a bit lost – I think I ended up on the school playing fields round the back and I saw someone waiting out there . . .'

Gina and Amy both looked at him expectantly,

hoping he had seen Min and that she was OK.

'Well,' he continued, wishing he'd mentioned this before now, 'he gave me a bit of a scare – hiding in some bushes wearing a nasty-looking mask.'

'Oh no!' Amy exclaimed. Suddenly she was beginning to feel really frightened.

'I think we should tell Mrs Knebworth,' Gina added anxiously.

'Not yet – wait here!' Amy instructed, then ran off, her cat tail swishing behind her.

'Wait here?' Dermot repeated. 'We need to get out there and look for Min.'

But within minutes Amy was back, along with two beefy Sixth Form girls armed with hockey sticks. Amy was also carrying three hockey sticks and matter-of-factly handed one to Dermot and one to Gina, keeping the third for herself.

'Right!' the beefiest sixth former, a girl called Helen, said with obvious relish. 'Ready to go and rescue Min?'

She pushed open the door to the kitchen and everyone else fell in behind her. A moment later, the four girls plus Dermot were out in the boarding-house garden.

It was dark outside. A damp and chilling Halloween dark.

'OK – we'll split up and circle the garden,' Helen instructed. 'Milly and I will go this way, you go the other – poke about in the bushes and call Min's name.'

'Min,' Gina shouted into the darkness, 'are you out here?'

The wind rustling in the many trees and bushes seemed to swallow her voice up immediately.

'C'mon,' Dermot urged, and the three of them moved forward and began to search in earnest.

Within a few minutes Dermot, Gina and Amy had made their way right round their half of the gardens; they were sure that Min was not there.

As Milly and Helen approached them, it was obvious they'd not seen anything either.

'Where did you think you saw this other person?' Gina asked Dermot.

'Behind the boarding house – out round the back on those playing fields,' he told her, pointing in the direction he'd come from at the start of the party.

'Let's get out there,' Amy said. She sounded braver than she felt. It was cold out here in the dark in just a cat costume, and despite the heavy stick in her hands, she felt scared – not just for herself, but for Min.

How *could* Min have been so stupid? Not to even

tell them she was thinking about doing something like this. It was insane!

As they headed out of the gardens, with a churn of fear, Amy saw something white flash in the trees ahead of them.

'What was that?' she said, hating the way she had grabbed Dermot's padded arm in fright.

'I don't know. Let's go and have a look,' he replied.

Both Amy and Gina couldn't help noticing how totally cool he sounded. Maybe if they were wearing several thick layers of foam rubber instead of tutus and tights, they would be feeling braver too.

They all went over to where Amy had seen the flash of white. Dermot delved into the undergrowth, and when he came out he was carrying something that made Amy recoil. It was one of those horrible masks – a ghostly white skull in a twisted silent scream.

'Oh!' Amy gasped.

'I did see someone wearing this earlier,' Dermot said, 'but they've obviously taken it off.'

'Maybe's Min's stalker is the prowler?' Gina wondered out loud, her voice tense.

Dermot tossed the mask over the wall into the gardens.

Amy turned to face the black blankness of the

school playing fields in front of them. Putting her hands up to cup her lips, she took a deep breath, then bellowed, '*Min!*' at the top of her voice. '*Miiiinnn!*' she shouted a second time.

They all waited in silence, desperate to hear any sort of reply above the trees, the wind and the other sounds of the night.

'Over there!' Helen said suddenly. She was pointing to the far side of the field, where a clump of trees marked the boundary of the school grounds.

The rest of the group strained their eyes to see if they could make anything out.

'There!' she repeated. 'There are two people over there. They're struggling!'

'Hurry!' Gina urged, and they all began to run towards the figures.

As they drew closer, the two figures, both dressed in black, became slightly clearer. Long dark hair, long dark dress – it was Min! Surely it was Min!

Min seemed to have spotted them and was trying to push the man with her away, but he grabbed her round the waist and buried his head against her neck.

At that, Amy found her courage. Lifting up her hockey stick, she began to sprint towards the figures, letting out a very scary, throaty, Glaswegian-sounding '*Aaaaaaaaaaaaargh!*'

Gina, Dermot and the sixth formers followed her lead. The man let go of Min as soon as he saw the group heading towards him, sticks at the ready. He turned and began to run away.

'*Aaaaaaaaargh! Arsehole!*' Amy screamed, charging on, furious at the thought of this louse, this lowlife, getting away from them.

'You look after Min!' Dermot was now outrunning Gina and Amy. 'We'll get him.'

So he, Helen and Milly raced across the playing field after the fleeing man while Amy and Gina ran towards Min.

Only when they were twenty metres away did they realize that it wasn't her at all. There, dressed in a clingy black dress and a gothy black wig, holding a wine bottle in one hand and a cigarette in the other, was a very annoyed-looking Mel.

'What the hell was all that about?' she demanded.

'Mel, you stupid tart!' Amy stormed.

'Oh, I'm the stupid tart! You've just frightened the living daylights out of Jono. I don't know where the bloody hell he's off to. Why are two jolly hockey sticks and a Shrek chasing after him? Hmm? What the hell is going on?'

'Oh, shut up, you stupid cow.' Amy was so angry and so worried, she really didn't have a second to be polite to anyone, especially Miss Melanie Where-are-my-knickers!

'We've lost Min,' Gina explained, on the verge of tears. 'We think she's out here with some stalker she's met on the Internet.'

'*What?*' Mel sounded incredulous. 'Min? I saw her about ten minutes ago. She was on a bench, over there' – she pointed towards the main school building – 'beside the school, chatting to some boy . . . A stalker?' She sounded almost impressed. 'He looked pretty harmless to me – but then you never can tell.'

Without another word Amy and Gina turned and began to run towards the main school building. As they rounded the corner where three benches over-looked the tennis courts, they immediately caught sight of the sleek dark head of their friend. She was deep in conversation with a boy!

Amy and Gina had almost reached the bench before Min and her friend turned towards them in surprise.

'*Min!*' Amy shrieked. 'We've been frantic!'

The boy stood up and looked at them nervously.

'It's OK, Greg, these are my friends,' Min assured him.

'Greg?' Gina asked. 'Are you the Gecko?'

Greg, who looked about fifteen or sixteen, just like them, had a friendly, freckly face surrounded by a thick mop of brown hair. He was dressed in jeans and a casual jacket over a T-shirt with a green lizard design on the front. Maybe this was how Min was supposed to recognize him or something.

He smiled at them shyly, before saying, 'Hello . . . Amy and Gina?'

'Yeah,' they replied together.

He certainly didn't look like a scary stalker. He looked sweet. He looked like just the kind of person Min would really like to hang out with.

'You should have told me!' Amy scolded Min. 'We thought you were out here with some stranger who tracked you down on the Internet!'

This made Min laugh. 'Well . . . it *was* a bit like that,' she joked.

'Oh, thanks,' Greg said.

'No! I'm joking,' Min told him. 'I think you can trust a boy who knows the value of pi to forty-two decimal places.' She couldn't stifle a giggle at this.

'Right, well, if you say so!' was Gina's baffled comment.

'I think you should know that Dermot and two sixth formers are out there somewhere chasing Mel's latest conquest – because they think he's your stalker,' Amy pointed out.

'Really?' Min was taken aback.

'I hope they're OK,' Gina added.

'I think Shrek can take care of himself,' Amy reassured her. She hugged her arms around herself, realizing how cold she was – and her *feet*: they were totally soaked through!

'You know,' she urged her friends, 'we're going to have to get back to the boarding house before Mrs K notices there's something going on. Dermot and co. might even be back by now.'

'Well, erm . . . nice to meet you,' Greg said to Amy and Gina.

'Yeah – we must do this again in daylight some time,' Amy teased.

But all Greg's attention had turned back to Min. 'Very nice to meet you, finally,' he told her, a broad smile breaking over his face. 'Would you like to come out with me next Saturday? We could—'

'*Yes!*' Min answered, before he could even finish.

He held out his hand for her to shake, but Min electrified her audience by leaning forward and kissing him on the cheek.

Amy so wanted to call out, *Wooooooo-hoooooo,* but she managed to restrain herself. This was Min. This was very fragile, tender territory. She couldn't step in and mess it all up.

'Goodnight,' Min said to Greg before he turned and walked off into the darkness.

Arm in arm, joking and teasing each other about the events of the last hour, the three girls made their way down onto the path back to the boarding house.

It was cold and windy now. The trees were making shadows dance across the playing field and it was impossible not to feel slightly spooked. Instinctively, the three hurried towards the cosy warmth of the party.

Past a clump of bushy shrubs they went, then into the house garden – where they saw a tall figure, shrouded in black, with the horrible scream mask covering its face, heading towards the house.

This was just too much for Amy: she couldn't stop herself from letting out a bloodcurdling scream, which stopped the figure in its tracks.

It turned and, to their horror, began to speed towards them.

'No! No! No!' Amy was gasping. '*Do* something!'

She pushed Gina, who was still holding a hockey stick, forward.

'Leave us alone,' Gina ordered in a shaky voice, her stick held across her body unconvincingly.

The figure kept on coming towards them.

'Go away!' Everyone could hear the terror in Gina's voice.

'I'm calling the police!' Min blurted out. 'Leave us alone.'

Then, to their horror, the figure began to laugh. It actually threw back its head and roared with laughter.

Just as both Gina and Min, their bodies shaking with fear, decided that this was the scariest thing they had ever witnessed and they were never leaving the house on Halloween or any other night, ever again, Amy let out a furious cry.

'Niffy!' she shouted. 'You hideous old bag! . . . *Niffy!*' she bellowed again, and started to march towards the figure.

Niffy? Gina and Min were still clutching each other, unable to believe that Amy was right.

But sure enough, the figure now said, 'OK! Take it easy,' in an oh-so-familiar plummy voice, and began to back away with her hands up.

No use.

Amy, absolutely livid, grabbed her friend by the shoulders and shook her. 'How *dare* you scare us,' she shouted, 'after the night *we've* had!'

'All right!' Niffy pushed Amy's hands away from her shoulders and pulled off the horrible mask.

They saw now that she wasn't in fancy dress at all. She was just wearing dark jeans, a jumper and a mac, with a bulky messenger bag slung across her body.

'I found the mask in the garden and I couldn't resist . . .' Niffy began. 'I know how scared you—'

'*Shut up!*' Amy instructed her. 'We've got quite enough on without you bloody showing up and giving us the scare of our lives.' The hairs on the back of her neck were still standing up and she felt as if they would never go down again.

'What on earth are you doing here, Niffy?' Min asked finally.

In a voice that managed to get almost all the way to the end of the sentence without too much of a wobble, Niffy began, 'I'm here, buddies, because my mum got her first all-clear today. I just jumped on the train because I knew, even though it's bonkers, that I had to tell . . . erm' – here was the wobble – 'tell you all in person.'

Chapter Twenty-eight

The front door of the boarding house burst open and teenagers, teachers, Mrs Knebworth – even the DJ – all began to rush out.

Word had spread. Milly, Helen and some younger girls were out on the playing fields trying to rescue someone! It had started as a whisper, grown to a rumour and then become a fully fledged panic.

On the dance floor the music had come to an abrupt halt as the plug was pulled out. Couples entangled in various cushioned areas were left red-faced as bright overhead lights were snapped on. Questions couldn't be answered quickly enough.

'A stalker?' Mrs Knebworth was booming. 'Asimina Singupta has a *stalker*?' She couldn't have sounded more incredulous. 'People are out there fighting with him? Good gracious!'

However, the Neb was made of stern Edinburgh

stuff. She hadn't flapped, she hadn't panicked. She'd calmly instructed the St Lennox teachers and several of the burliest Frankensteins, Draculas and mad monks to get out there and discover what was going on.

But now here was Min, making her way through the crowds of people towards the boarding house, apparently completely calm and unruffled.

'Where on earth have you girls been?' Mrs Knebworth boomed at the Irises as soon as she spotted them. 'And Luella Nairn-Bassett?' she added, her eyebrows shooting up almost into her hair. 'What in the name of goodness are you doing here?'

But before the question could be answered, there were loud shouts and a series of cheers from the far corner of the garden.

Dermot and the two sixth formers were coming towards the house. All three looked a little the worse for wear. The girls were muddy, with ruffled hair, but Dermot's Shrek costume was completely mangled. Half of his face mask had torn away and his eye was swollen and bleeding.

Gina ran across the garden towards them. 'Are you all OK?' she asked them, but she had eyes only for Dermot's battered face. 'Did he attack you?' she exclaimed.

'No, no,' Dermot assured her. 'I'm just a total pillock who took a tumble.'

'We chased him towards the embankment,' Helen explained, 'but he got away and then Dermot lost his footing.'

'You fell down the *embankment*?' Gina asked. She had once gone to the school's boundary fence and looked down there. It was a long steep drop.

'Thank goodness for the padding,' Dermot said, patting his costume, 'or things would have been a lot nastier for me down at the bottom.'

'You rolled all the way down?' Gina asked again.

'I know . . . total pillock,' Dermot added.

But nevertheless, Gina slipped her hand into his and squeezed it hard.

Amy was standing beside them now. 'Unfortunately you were chasing Mel's boyfriend, not Min's stalker.'

'You've got to stop calling him that,' Min chipped in. 'I'm never, ever going to live this down.'

'What!' Milly exclaimed. 'Mel's boyfriend! But we've even got his shoe!' She held up a muddied white trainer.

'Let me take a look at that!' Mrs Knebworth was out in the garden now.

She took hold of the trainer and brought it up to

the light at the front door. After a close inspection of the sole, she announced to everyone who would listen – everyone who wasn't already talking, asking, answering, describing or speculating – 'I think we've found our prowler! Will everyone who knows anything about all this come into my sitting room right now?' she ordered. 'And everyone else' – she looked at the large group of teenagers spread out over her garden, trampling the flowers, scuffing the lawn, stamping over the newly dug beds – 'get straight back inside and *party*, for heaven's sake!'

In the midst of the noisy, thronging crowd making its way from the garden back into the boarding house, Gina turned to Dermot. They gazed at each other, their fingers linked together, and just like in the sculpture gardens, it no longer mattered who else was there. They were alone together.

There was no Scarlett, Gina realized with a fizzy rush of happiness. There was just Dermot, and he was so, *so* into her! And that, she realized as she felt his warm mouth pressed against hers, was something very special. Something very well worth having.

When the kiss finally ended, Dermot leaned in against her ear and whispered, 'Eat your heart out, Scarlett!'

Gina couldn't think of anything to say, so she just settled for kissing his salty and slightly muddy neck instead.

'I quite like you,' Dermot breathed against the side of her head.

'I really quite like you too,' she told him back.

'Gina Peterson!'

Gina was vaguely aware that the Neb was calling her name.

'My sitting room!' the housemistress instructed. 'And Olly Hughes better bring himself along as well.'

There was a lecture, of course. All about leaving the boarding house without permission and making friends on the Internet, and did they have any idea what danger they'd placed themselves in tonight? But, funnily enough, it didn't seem to last long.

Mrs Knebworth seemed most distracted by the battered and bleeding Shrek in the corner of her sitting room. She kept catching sight of him and losing the thread of her tirade. Finally she just threw up her arms and said, 'Well, we've all lived to tell the tale. Now, you, mister, need some TCP on that cut. Milly, bring me the first-aid box. Gina and Min, make yourselves useful and get a round of tea in here for everyone.'

When the cut had been cleaned, Gina and Dermot sat side by side on the sofa holding hands. Niffy and Amy were squeezed together on the armchair opposite, chatting and joking, delighted to be together again.

Suddenly Amy realized that there was something her friend should know: she sat up and informed Niffy, 'Angus is here! He's here, at the party. You have to go and find him. He'll want to know about your mum . . .'

'What!'

Niffy sprang up; then, as she got to her feet, she remembered something and dipped a hand into the back pocket of her jeans. 'Oh, Aim, I've got something for you,' she announced. 'You left it at Blacklough and I kept meaning to tell you . . . or send it on or something, but you know what I'm like!'

She held out her hand, and Amy screamed when she saw her precious palm tree-shaped, diamond-studded necklace glinting there.

'Niffy! You total tit!' she shrieked, pretending to smack her friend on the head. 'I've been searching everywhere for my necklace! Everywhere! The whole boarding house was on alert. And you . . . you've been carrying my *diamonds* about in your scruffy old denims! Unbelievable!'

Shrek looked at Gina. He was beginning to think that really, anything could happen next. Swivelling round in his great foamy costume, which he still hadn't been able to take off because he was only wearing boxers underneath, he got hold of his brown bag. Opening the flap, he looked inside – but there was no hiding his utter disappointment. 'The pie . . .' he began.

'Ohmigod, the pumpkin pie!' Gina turned to look inside the bag now.

Dermot and the Shrek costume had squidged that lovingly home-made pie into a sticky, soggy mess.

Surveying the disaster inside the bag, Dermot decided he would just close the flap on it and deal with it another day.

'He brought you a pumpkin pie?' Min asked as she handed round the mugs of tea.

'He *made* me a pumpkin pie.' Gina beamed.

'Now that is sweet, that is really sweet . . .' Min told him.

Mrs Knebworth leaned over to Gina and patted her

arm. 'That's a very nice boy you have there, that Olly Hughes.'

'Yes!' Gina smiled at Dermot. 'Very nice!'

'You'll have to introduce him to your mother when she comes.'

'Yes!' Gina added mischievously. 'I will.'

'Your *mum*?' Dermot asked, and there was no hiding the nerves in his voice. 'So when's she coming to Scotland?'

'My mum plus my three oldest best friends, Ria, Paula and Maddison . . .' Gina began.

She looked over at the little gold carriage clock on Mrs K's mantelpiece. 'They'll be here . . . oh . . . in about thirteen hours. But don't worry! My mum is going to *love* you, Olly!'

MEET THE AUTHOR . . .

CARMEN

Full name: Carmen Maria Reid

Home: A creaky Victorian house
in Glasgow, Scotland

Likes: Writing (luckily), chocolate in any shape
or form especially if caramel is involved, Jack
Russell dogs, cute blue-eyed guys in glasses,
children (especially hers), buying handbags,
holidays by the sea, Earl Grey tea in
an insulated mug, very very long walks,
very, very long jeans, shepherd's pie,
hot bubble baths (for inspiration), duvet coats,
playing tennis

Dislikes: Large animals, drinking milk (bleurrrrgh),
high heels (she's already 6ft 1), going to the gym
(but she goes anyway), filling in forms or
paperwork of any kind, flying

Would like to be: The author of lots more books
(Secret ambition was to be a ballet dancer or
Olympic gold medal winning runner)

Fascinating fact: Carmen spent four years
boarding at a girls' school very like St J's

Secrets at St Jude's

New Girl

By Carmen Reid

Ohmigod! Gina's mum has finally flipped and is sending her to Scotland to some crusty old *boarding school* called St Jude's – just because Gina spent all her money on clothes and got a few bad grades! It's so *unfair!*

Now the Californian mall-rat has to swap her sophisticated life of pool parties and well-groomed boys for . . . hockey *in the rain*, school dinners and stuffy housemistresses. And what's with her three kooky dorm-buddies . . . could they ever be her *friends?* And just how does a St Jude's girl get out to meet the gorgeous guys invited to the school's summer ball?

978 0 552 55706 1

www.rbooks.co.uk

JUMPING TO CONFUSIONS
by LIZ RETTIG

I'm Cat – and I'm the fat, plain one in my family. When I say fat, I don't mean 'have-to-be-prised-out-of-a-hula-hoop' fat, but when your mum and sister are practically size zero, it's hard not to feel like elephant girl in comparison.

My twin sister Tessa is blonde, gorgeous and gets any boy she wants. Right now she's got her eye on Josh, a really fit American guy who's just moved to Glasgow. But he doesn't seem interested in her. It's weird. I've never known any boy who didn't fancy Tessa. Well, not any straight ones anyway . . .

Of course! It all makes sense . . . Funny that he doesn't want to tell anyone his secret, not even me, his new best friend . . .

Could Cat be jumping to conclusions about Josh?

A wonderfully funny tale of romantic confusion from the author of My Desperate Love Diary

ISBN: 978 0 552 557573

EXTREME KISSING
BY LUISA PLAJA

Two best friends. One extreme adventure.
Too many secrets . . .

Bethany is the sensible one with a long-term boyfriend, Carlota is the rebellious one with the wild past. All is fine in their world – except Carlota hates her step-dad and longs for her ex. And Bethany is worried that her boyfriend is about to dump her - and she's 'late' . . .

Carlota has a plan to put their troubles behind them on a crazy day out in London. She uses her favourite magazine to guide them on a life-changing adventure – setting real challenges from the glossy pages that lead to exclusive shopping, exciting snogging and . . . explosive secrets. The magazine will take them everywhere they need to go - but will it make them reveal the truths they are keeping from each other?

ISBN: 978 0 552 55681 1

SELINA PENALUNA
by JAN PAGE

Selina Penaluna is a merrymaid – or so she believes . . .

Dropped as a baby into a deep pool on the Cornish shore, she emerges a different child – a mermaid changeling – and is forever drawn to the sea. Abandoned by her mother, neglected and abused by her father, she desperately wants to escape her lonely life.

Ellen and Jack are twins, evacuated from East London to Cornwall at the start of the war. The family that takes them in are well-off and a little stuffy. Ellen relishes this opportunity to better herself, but Jack finds his new life stifling and seeks freedom in the arms of Selina, the mysterious fisherman's daughter whose wild beauty turns every man's head.

Selina's siren song has Jack captivated – but leaves his sister cold with jealousy. Can the young lovers find solace and build a new life together? And how will Ellen deal with being left behind?

A spellbinding, beautiful novel full of passion and tragedy that will enchant older readers.

ISBN: 978 0 552 55864 8